They are

Coming

They are Coming

Christopher Mlalazi

WEAVER
PRESS

Published by Weaver Press, Box A1922, Avondale, Harare. 2014
<www.weaverpresszimbabwe.com>

© Christopher Mlalazi, 2014

Typeset by Weaver Press
Cover Design: Design Duo, Harare
Cover illustration: Calvin Chimutuwah
Printed by: Directory Publishers, Harare and Bulawayo

ISBN: 978-1-77922-258-9

CHRISTOPHER MLALAZI is currently Guest Writer of the City of Hanover in Germany, the most recent of a series of writing fellowships. In 2012, he was a fellow at the Iowa International Writing Program, USA; in 2011, he was Guest Writer at the Nordic Africa Institute in Sweden; and, in 2010, Guest Writer at Villa Aurora, in Los Angeles, USA. Prolific as a prose writer and playwright, in 2008 he was the co-winner of the Oxfam Novib PEN Freedom of Expression Award at the Hague for theatre. He won NAMA awards for his short story collection, *Dancing With Life: Tales From The Township* and for his play *Election Day*. His second novel, *Running with Mother*, has been translated into German and Italian.

2004

Chapter 1

'A woman who sweeps her yard after the sun has risen will make a bad wife,' Ambition's mother used to tell Senzeni whenever she was late up. Her brother knew why: You're happy when you dream of nice things. But, today, although it's the school holidays, and he does not have to sweep the yard, which is the duty of women, Ambition has woken up very early after a restless night as if someone, somewhere, was trying to tell him something.

Standing at the gate, he looks down Sibambene Street. The sun has just risen, promising another warm autumn day. His mother has already swept their yard, and is now busy washing the dishes by the door. '*Hawu*, up so early Ambi, what's the matter?' Ambition rubbed his eyes and yawned, 'Nothing, Mama, my sleep is gone.'

'Then you must be missing school, my child.' His mother smiled, her eyes glancing over him, as if checking, as only a mother can, to see if her son has woken up any taller. 'Don't worry, the holiday will soon be over and you'll be back with your books again.' She gathers her dishes and goes into the house.

Lobengula Township sprawls over a series of rises in the western townships of Bulawayo. Named after last King of the Ndebele, it can be clearly seen on the skyline from Luveve, Magwegwe, Njube and Emakhandeni. Ambition and his family stay on the northernmost rise, the one that

1

faces towards Luveve and Emakhandeni.

Although it's early, a radio is already blasting gangster music from one of the houses along the street. Ambition knows it's 3Pac's. He's the one who's always the first to switch on his radio. 3Pac was a strange man. Gangster music, Ambition thought, was not for men his age. He should be listening to traditional music like *imbube*, which his father liked.

He can also hear the shouts of children playing 'hit me,' and guessed Ntando must be with them, for his friend was always an early riser, sometimes sitting outside Ambition's door waiting for him to wake up to go and play.

A few women – one, two, three, four, five: one big mother and four thin mothers – are sweeping the five yards of their five houses after the sun has risen. Five bad wives. Suddenly, MaVundla stops and pulls herself upright. She's the big one whom his father says is too clever by half. She looks in his direction. Even at a distance, Ambition can see that her mouth has opened in surprise or shock.

Then she turns to her neighbour, a woman Ambition does not know as she's only recently arrived in their line. MaVundla seems to say something and the other woman jerks upright and they both stare in his direction. Then, one by one, from both sides of the street, all the sweeping women straighten up and stare at him.

Ambition's mind races. Has MaVundla gossiped about him, or his family, or Senzeni, and so early in the morning, although the way they're standing seems to suggest something else? They appear poised, as if about to drop their sweeps and explode into their houses. But they also look as if they're playing Statue, and only waiting for Ambition to call 'relax' so they can continue their work.

When a call comes, it does so from behind him, and it's the cry of an adult, *'They're coming!'*

He turns. A man is running towards him.

It's Mr Nkani, the bald teacher who left Lobengula II High at the end of the year, whose picture is on some of the election posters now pasted all over the township. People say he wants to be an MP for the MDC.

As he draws closer, Ambition sees blood flowing down the left side of his face. It's stained his shirt as if somebody has sprayed him with raspberry juice. 'Run! Hide!' Mr Nkani shouts as he races past him. 'They're behind me!'

'Ambition!' his mother screams from the open window of the kitchen, dread on her face. 'Quick! Come into the house!' Ntando's chubby face appears beside his mother, his eyes seem huge with fear.

'No, Mama.' Ambition hitches up his sagging shorts.

'No!' MaNdlovu's face disappears from the window.

Ambition looks down the street. There's nobody in sight. Mr Nkani and the sweeping women have disappeared.

He looks up the street, as a gang of youths turn into it running hard and in silence. Only the fury of their pounding feet and pumping arms signals their intention. Green Bombers in green T-shirts. The country's flag streams above them as if they're accompanied by a brightly coloured bird.

His mother appears behind him, snatches him up in both hands, and runs into the house with him, as if he were weightless.

So, Ambition now peers at the action through the kitchen window, as if he were watching a forbidden movie on television. His mother is beside him, her mouth rigid with fear; Ntando is on the other side, his face pressed against the glass, and Ambition can feel excitement radiating off his body.

The Green Bombers zip past the gate. Nobody needs to be told whom they want to catch today.

***

Ambition, Ntando and some friends had been returning from a soccer game in Luveve Township just a week previously when they'd seen the Green Bombers near Lobengula Hall. They'd been chasing a man and a woman wearing MDC T-shirts, just as they were chasing Mr Nkani now. The couple had been caught in front of their eyes and had been kicked and stomped on until, covered in blood, they lay on the ground as if dead.

Senzeni had been with the Green Bombers then, although she hadn't taken part in the beating, perhaps because she'd been carrying their flag. She'd shouted at Ambition and his friends to vamoose. Some of his friends had run away immediately, but Ambition and Ntando had only moved a short distance, and then, spellbound, continued to watch the action. Afterwards, the two boys walked home in a dazed silence. The violence had been brutal.

When Ambition reached home, he hadn't told his mother what he'd seen or that Senzeni had been with the Green Bombers; instead, he'd taken out his King Kong book to read under the mulberry tree in the backyard.

Chapter 2

Now that the Green Bombers have passed, Ambition, evading his mother, slips out of the door, and crouching at the gate, looks down the street. The Green Bombers have disappeared, just like Mr Nkani and the sweeping women. He straightens up as, one by one, men, women and children come out of their houses and stare down the silent road. He can see MaVundla's big frame at her gate, her son Power next to her.

No one speaks. The gangster music has stopped. It's as if its lifeblood had been swallowed. Suddenly, they hear screams, and people disappear, again at lightning speed, banging their doors closed behind them.

The Green Bombers have reappeared, running hard, but this time they seem to be running away from something. Again Ambition is unceremoniously carted aloft in his mother's arms, and deposited back in the kitchen.

'Stubborn! You are!' MaNdlovu shouts, as she slams the door closed and locks it, before peering through the window, Ambition and Ntando beside her again.

The Green Bombers flee past, as if hurled from a catapult. There's a brief lull, and then another group zips past the window, hard on their heels.

This new group is giving chase, yelling and whistling, unlike the Green Bombers who had been silent as they chased after Mr Nkani. It's a mixture of men, women, children, and the township stray, Ginger. Normally a timid dog, he's barking and running alongside them as if it were the most exciting day of his life.

Mr Nkani, now shirtless, is leading these people, snatching up stones from the ground and throwing them towards the Green Bombers as he runs. Without a thought, Ambition unlocks and opens the back door and runs around the house to the gate, his mother yelling after him in a mixture of fury and anxiety.

Other people have joined the chase. He even sees MaVundla, her breasts bouncing up and down under her blouse, with Power running slightly in front of her.

Ambition can't resist, and he joins the running crowd, his arms pumping. But all of a sudden the people in front of him turn around, and start pelting back the way they've come. Ambition is pushed to the side, and suddenly he finds himself right in the path of the Green Bombers. Fortunately, they suddenly pull to a stop, and Ambition stares at them across a thin stream of effluent. Complete silence has descended.

Ambition's eyes focus on Senzeni. She's wearing a green floppy hat over her green T-shirt and trousers, and she's holding a flag.

'Senzeni!' Ambition shouts, 'What do you think you're doing?'

His sister simply points at him with her flagstaff. 'Get out of our way or you'll get hurt!' she yells.

'Ambition!' He hears his mother's voice.

The silence is broken. The Green Bombers yell and stones start flying, but Ambition and his mother are not the target. It's the people massed behind them, who respond fiercely. Flying stones fill the air. Ambition finds himself being dragged by the hand down the side of the street, his mother muttering about how he obviously wants to get them all killed.

Back at the window again, they're all staring out at a now dead street, when a bicycle skids into their yard and falls over in a rattle of metal and spinning wheels. A man leaps off, and moments later Ambition's father is beside them at the window.

'You're not hurt?' MaNdlovu's voice cracks with worry.

'I'm not.' Ngwenya shakes his head. He's breathing hard. Dressed in dark overalls, he peers intently through the window, as if whatever was behind him might appear and follow him inside his own house. 'But they nearly got me. Has there been any sign of Senzeni?'

'No. Nothing,' MaNdlovu's shoulders droop.

'I saw her,' Ambition looks up at his father.

'Where?'

'Today.'

'Where? Answer my question!'

'Please, don't shout at the child.' MaNdlovu turns to Ambition. 'Where did you see your sister, Ambi?'

'She was carrying the flag for the Green Bombers.'

A heavy silence descends on the room.

'She wasn't with them, Ambition,' his mother says softly. 'I saw the militia.' She turns to Ngwenya. 'He's mistaken, he must've seen someone who looks like Senzeni.'

'It was her,' Ambition says stubbornly. 'I told her she was making a mistake.'

'Don't answer your mother back!'

'Don't snap at the child, Ngwenya.'

'It's you who spoils the children!'

'What have *I* done?'

'You contradict me when I try to discipline them. That's why Senzeni is doing what she's doing now!'

'Don't blame me for your failures!' MaNdlovu blazes.

Before Ngwenya can respond, Ambition darts to the door, opens it, and runs out. It bangs closed.

His mother's cry follows him, 'Come back, Ambition!', as the boy slips through a hole in the *delele* hedge between his home and Ntando's.

Tracked by the white-hot eye of the mid-morning sun, he runs across Ntando's backyard. There's nobody in sight, only the shirt and trousers of a police uniform hanging on a washing line, looking like an upside-down officer. Gangster music is blasting over the township again.

Ambition squeezes through another hole in the hedge on the other side of the yard and into MaVundla's property. There's no one there either, and he quickly runs past a vegetable garden flooded with sewer effluent.

Slipping through the strands of a wire fence on the other side, he observes MaVundla standing before the open door of the house from which the music is pouring. Looking angry, she's holding a pair of children's black school shoes in one hand and a cigarette in the other. 3Pac comes out, a cap back to front on his head, a bottle of beer in one hand.

'I want my money right now!' MaVundla yells at him.

'Bring those shoes back before I *hit* you!' 3Pac shouts above the noise of the music, waving his bottle at her. 'How many times have I told you that they belong to a client?'

3Pac and MaVundla are so angry with each other that even though Ambition is in full view, they show no sign of having seen him.

'You're going to hit your grandmother's buttocks not me!' MaVundla points at him with her cigarette. 'What kind of a man are you that picks up women and then fails to pay them after you've satisfied yourself?'

'I'll hit you if you don't watch your mouth!'

'Hee-hee-hee!' MaVundla laughs shrilly. 'Hit me and see what'll happen to you, boy!' She throws the cigarette at him, and 3Pac's bottle flies at her. Quick as a flash, MaVundla ducks, and the bottle whizzes past Ambition's head. Seeing the bottle miss his target, 3Pac leaps at MaVundla and she races away, the old man in hot pursuit. As she runs, she yells, 'I want my money! My body is not for free!'

'Prostitute!' 3Pac shouts as he chases after her. He's running as if he's wet his trousers, legs wide, one hand gripping his trousers by the belt as if they might fall down. Pursuer and pursued disappear around the house, as Ambition runs across the yard and climbs over the fence.

Finally, he emerges into Sibambene Street, six houses away from his home. He walks fast, heading east past pockets of people, mostly agitated women talking in hushed tones.

He walks purposefully on, until he emerges into Masiyephambili Drive. He waits for a long distance haulage truck to roar past, and then skips to the other side. He's in a small bushy area between Lobengula and Njube townships, where a tall *marula* tree provides shade. An Apostolic Faith Church group is congregated there. Ambition heads towards them.

Chapter 3

The congregation is not very large; its members, all singing, are kneeling before the priest in neat rows, their white gowns contrasting with the monotony of the earth colours of the autumn bush. When the priest, Siziba, sees Ambition, he raises his long staff over his head, as if he wants to hook something above him. The singing stops immediately. Ambition stops before him and hitches up his shorts.

The priest regards him silently. He's an elderly man with a clean-shaven head and a long white beard. A huge red cross is stitched to the front of his gown.

'You're late today,' Siziba's voice is low and grating. 'It's past eleven now.'

'There were Green Bombers in the street,' Ambition replies. 'My mother didn't want me to leave the house.'

'We saw the fighting from here,' Siziba acknowledges. 'Has your sister returned home?'

Ambition shakes his head. 'No.'

'When did you last see her?'

'She was with the Green Bombers today.'

Siziba raises his face to the sky, closes his eyes, and breaks into a song. The congregation do the same. Still singing, Siziba hands his Bible and staff to the woman kneeling beside him, his wife MaSiziba. Beside her is MaChivanda, the money-changer who lives in the big yellow house behind Ambition's home.

Then, stretching his arms towards Ambition, his eyes half-closed, the priest flicks his fingers in and out, beckoning him nearer. Ambition steps forward and kneels in front of Siziba, who grips his face in both his hands, and looking up to the heavens breaks into tongues, while the women sing.

MaChivanda is leading in a light but beautiful descant.

Ambition feels Siziba's palms on his cheeks squeezing them so that his lips pout. It makes him feel silly. Given a choice, he would have preferred the priest to place his hands on his head, as he does with the adults.

Finally, the prayer ends, and Siziba joins in the singing again, smoothly taking the lead from MaChivanda. Removing his hands from Ambition's cheeks, he takes a strip of red cloth from a bag at his feet and, still singing, he ties it around the boy's forehead. Then he takes a length of white cloth from the bag, pours a little water on it, and hands the cloth to Ambition.

'Go there and face towards the source of the evil, my son,' the priest instructs, pointing at a slab of rock. 'Cover yourself with this cloth and pray to the Lord to make your sister see reason and return home.'

With the red band around his forehead, and without a shirt, Ambition feels like a WWF champion. He kneels on the slab of rock, the white cloth draped over his small shoulders, its ends in his hands. He has not yet covered his head to pray. The scene before him is too interesting. His mind wanders.

The land rises slowly toward the houses on the other side of the Masiyephambili Road. To the left is the Lobengula Beer Garden, which is built on the rise in such a way that it seems as if it is sliding backwards towards him. Ambition can see that people are assembled in a group in the middle of the garden, in the space reserved for dancing, just in front of the jukebox. But there's no music coming from there today, no rumba, no Solomon Skhuza, the beer garden patrons' preferred music.

Adjacent to the beer garden is Ilanga Youth Centre where the Green Bombers have their camp. Unusually, there is no activity inside its barbed wire fenced grounds.

A group of people emerge from behind the beer garden. Ambition instantly recognises their green T-shirts. He squints hard trying to see Senzeni, but it is far too far away to see any one individual. So he looks for the flag, and can't see that either.

A police truck comes to a stop beside the Green Bombers. Police officers jump out, and the two groups engage in conversation. Ambition looks back to the beer garden. The group there seems to be being addressed by a man in a white shirt. Ambition wonders if it could be Mr Nkani. Then the Green Bombers turn away from the policemen and run into the township.

Ambition bends his head again, knowing he should be praying for Senzeni. He wonders if the priest is watching him.

***

Ambition heard that Mr Nkani was entering politics when his father had complained to his mother, and he'd been surprised. Not Mr Nkani! Not the weak-bodied teacher from Lobengula II High, whom the children in both the primary and secondary schools called Airport because of the bald patch on his head!

It had been after supper some months back, and Ambition had been lying on his parent's bed, half asleep, while they were still in the kitchen. His mother was sitting on the floor weaving a reed mat. His father was on the faded sofa doing nothing after a long day and a bad back. 'We send our kids to school to learn, but now those same teachers are holding secret meetings that will get the country into trouble,' he complained.

'We must buy cards for both parties,' his mother responded practically. 'A day will come when the youth will conduct door-to-door searches and we need to be prepared!'

'I won't waste my hard-earned money on such foolishness,' his father replied. 'I don't mend shoes all day sitting on a rock to spend my money on party cards!'

'This isn't about politics, Ambition's father, it's about survival.'

'Okay, so what if you mistakenly produce the wrong card?'

'We'll be careful. We'll keep them separately. I'll keep one and you the other.'

'So, which one will you keep, and which one will I be made to keep?'

'Ah, Ambition's father, that doesn't matter. We wouldn't be saying that we're now voting for them, or that we've become members of their party. Like I said, we'll just be doing it to make sure they don't bother us. We have to think for our children.'

'Okay, buy the cards then, but you keep them both. I don't want to have anything to do with such nonsense,' Ngwenya said firmly. 'Why should we be afraid of our own political parties when they're supposed to ensure that we live in peace? And that Mr Nkani is now one of them, too.'

Ambition's ears pricked up.

'I've heard that,' his mother said. 'He's been given a position in the MDC, and now wants to be an MP.'

'But how can a schoolteacher be involved in politics?' his father asked.

'A teacher needs time to plan his work so his pupils can pass their exams. If Mr Nkani enters politics, where's he going to get the time for his schoolwork? I ask you, should we be surprised when Senzeni comes home with bad marks!'

'Our daughter was not doing well long before Mr Nkani became involved in politics, Ngwenya,' His mother put a stop to the conversation, knowing that once her husband had a bee in his bonnet, she'd have to listen to him for a long time.

Ambition could hardly wait to go to school to break the news that something was soon going to happen to Mr Nkani. Politics was a dangerous game. Didn't his father always say that? And everyone knew that you didn't play around with ZANU-PF.

But imagining that Mr Nkani had the heart to risk his life was indeed surprising. The teacher was not known for his bravery.

Ambition remembered an athletics competition, when Mr Nkani had almost been beaten up by Mrs Gumbo, his class teacher. With his students watching, Mr Nkani had run away when Mrs Gumbo attacked him. Undeterred, she'd chased him round the athletics ground. At last, Mr Nkani ran to the primary school and hid in the office and the headmaster had to placate the angry Mrs Gumbo.

Ambition never found out the real reason why Mrs Gumbo had wanted to beat up Mr Nkani; there'd been so many rumours he just didn't know what to believe. One theory was that Mrs Gumbo was just a bully who wanted to make trouble for Mr Nkani. Certainly, Mrs Gumbo didn't need any big excuse to beat students in class.

Another, the juiciest, was that Mr Nkani had entered the ladies' toilet by mistake and without knocking and had found Mrs Gumbo with her pants down. But this rumour came from Power and Ambition hadn't believed it, as Power was famous for telling lies. Besides, thought Ambition, how do you enter a ladies' toilet by mistake?

But despite the stories, and meek as he was, Mr Nkani had been given a position in the MDC, and Ambition was sure that trouble would follow like a shadow.

Chapter 4

Ambition blinks his eyes and shakes his head, returning himself to the present. He knows he should quickly finish praying and go home, as his mother will be angry with him for running away without saying where he was going.

But he quickly sneaks another look at the drama unfolding before him, as one of the police officers peers over the beer garden wall at the group assembled inside. He returns to the other officers, and after a moment's conversation all the policemen turn towards the wall, and Ambition hears a soft popping sound. A moment later, smoke envelops the patrons.

There's no visible sign of a fire, but the group in the beer garden scatter, as if they've been flung hither and thither by a giant hand, and the police are chasing the men who've leapt over the wall and are trying to escape.

One of the police officers blocks the path of a man running towards him, wiping his eyes. The man stops running and raises his hands in surrender. It's the man in the white shirt, the one who'se been addressing the crowd, the one Ambition thought looked like Mr Nkani.

Ignoring his gesture, the policeman trips up his victim and lays into him with his truncheon; the man is screaming and rolling on the ground as he tries to evade the weapon, which descends on him again and again.

Then another man appears behind the policeman and kicks him hard. The officer loses his balance and falls to the ground. His victim leaps to his feet and he and his rescuer race away round the corner.

'Cover yourself and pray, Ambition!' Siziba shouts from behind him.

Ambition quickly kneels down on the rock and covers his head with the cloth. Its dampness feels cool on his body, but he still can't pray. Instead his mind replays the fighting outside the beer garden, and the smoke that had risen over it, and which he'd noticed had been drifting in his direction.

This is Ambition's fourth visit to Siziba's church. The first time had been at MaChivanda's invitation: 'We have a church service in my house tonight,' she'd told him. 'You must come and pray for your sister. God takes care of every problem in this world.'

He had told his mother about the invitation, excited at the prospect, but had not told her that he was going to pray for Senzeni. 'No!' his mother had declared. 'I won't have any child of mine attending that kind of a church.'

But after spending the afternoon playing street soccer, Ambition had slipped into the church service; his mother had thought he was still with his friends, and his father was still at the beer garden where he went every evening after work.

MaChivanda's living room that night had been packed with the white-gowned congregation, some children, and the long-bearded priest leading the service. During the praying and singing, Ambition had trouble keeping his eyes open, but he was suddenly pulled wide awake when he found himself lying in the middle of the floor, the skirts of the congregation whirling around him in dizzying circles, and Siziba kneeling over him praying fervently in tongues, his hands pressed on Ambition's cheeks.

'The Holy Spirit spoke through you, my son,' Siziba informed him in an exultant voice, as if a miracle had descended upon the room.

'How?' Ambition asked puzzled and confused, as the chanting congregation whirled around the room.

'Don't worry about how, but the Holy Spirit made one request. You must pray hard for your family and everything will be all right. Hallelujah!'

'Hallelujah!' the congregation chorused while MaChivanda nodded, looking complacent.

Siziba had dipped his fingers into a bowl on the floor beside him and sprinkled cold water over Ambition's face. It made him gasp.

Ambition never told his mother, but there and then he'd made the decision to join Siziba's church; not as a full member, but only to pray for his sister. Whenever Senzeni recovered from whatever was afflicting her and returned home, he would then leave the church. In the meantime he thought it was his responsibility to do something to make her better.

***

Ambition mumbles 'Amen' and throws back the cloth. The sun's sudden glare makes him squint. He ties the ends of the white cloth around his neck so that it hangs down his back like a cape.

He suddenly hears a cacophony of coughs and snorting and looks behind him – it's the congregation. Siziba seems to be the hardest hit, as he kneels on the ground, coughs racking his body. Staring in incomprehension, Ambition feels a burning sensation in his nostrils and in his throat, and he feels as if he were choking. His eyes are burning, but through a blur of tears, he sees Siziba rise, holding his stave in one hand, the Bible aloft in the other while incantations pour out of him, tears course down his cheeks and snot dribbles from his nose.

'Hold him!' Siziba suddenly commands the congregation. 'It is coming from him and it's powerful.' He spits.

Slowly, still coughing, the congregation move towards Ambition, but he zips past them, his white cloth flying from his shoulders like a Superman cape. He runs across the bush towards the road. He trips and falls over a stone. Driven by an inexplicable fear, he leaps up and continues running, dust covering his body. He can barely see, as the burning sensation in his eyes has intensified.

At last, he reaches the road. Blurred figures seem to be running everywhere around him. There is chaos. Cars horns blare, brakes squeal, as he runs across Masiyephambili Drive.

A car swerves, just missing him, its windscreen smashed to cobwebs; another car sweeps past, its bonnet heavily dented. He runs on. Then hands seize him and he feels himself borne into the air.

'No! No!' He struggles, realising that he can't see properly now. 'Put me down!' He closes his eyes, trying to refresh them.

'What's the matter with you?' It's a male voice, but thankfully not Siziba's.

He continues trying to free himself, as a feeling of nausea overcomes him.

'Be still, Ambition! I'm only trying to help you!'

There's something familiar about the voice, so he stops struggling. He tries to open his eyes, but they burn so much that he instantly closes them again.

They're moving, and he's being carried like a small child. After a while, he hears a door creak open.

'What's he wearing?' This voice is so deeply familiar it's as if it's a part of him. '*Mayiwe!* And why is he covered in dust? People have bewitched my child!' The voice rises. It's his mother!

'I picked him up at the main road, MaNdlovu. It looked as if he was running for his life!'

'Thank you, thank you, but please come into the bedroom and put him on the bed! You say he was running away – what from?'

'I don't know, I couldn't see anything behind him.'

'This is the work of witches! What do they want from us, please tell me?'

Ambition feels the white cloth tugged from his shoulders, and fingers are untying the red bandanna from around his forehead. His body feels sore.

'He's lucky to be alive!' says the male voice, which he still can't place. 'I saw him run across Masiyephambili Drive, cars racing past. They missed him by inches!'

'No!'

'If I'd not been there...'

'But where did he find these things he's wearing? Oh God, what's happening in this house?'

'That I cannot answer, Mama. Excuse me, but I have to go now. Mother has sent us money and I have to pick it up at Western Union.'

'Thank you, Freeman, for rescuing my son.' Ambition feels a wave of relief. It's Ntando's brother.

The door closes, and they hear footsteps walking to the gate.

Then the sound of sobbing fills the room.

'What have we done, spirits of Ngwenya and you of Ndlovu?' His mother's low voice comes to him between her sobs. 'Please take a careful look at us. Please look at how poor we are. Do we deserve all this sorrow?'

Chapter 5

At sunset, MaNdlovu, in her yellow dress and a black wool hat with its white Nike logo, walks along the deserted Sibambene Street with Ambition – who is really too big to be carried – on her back.

The street is deserted, but she's just passed the milkman parking his cart in front of MaVundla's house, before going in through the gate, a strange thing in itself because milkmen did their rounds in the morning, not at this late hour. MaNdlovu quickly dismisses the thought; now is not the time to dwell on such trivial matters.

To her left, the setting sun beams over the rooftops, as if curious to see what's happening in the township. MaNdlovu knows very well why the streets are deserted, but it hasn't stopped her.

When Freeman left, she'd inspected her son closely as he lay on the bed. He seemed uninjured, except for the film of dust that covered him. She worried that his eyes were bloodshot, as if he had a fever, but when she had felt his forehead, his temperature seemed normal. She'd asked him what the matter was, and Ambition told her drowsily that he was not feeling well, and just wanted to sleep.

She'd asked him where he'd got the red headband and the white cloth cape but the boy had just mumbled something incomprehensible. MaNdlovu had not pressed him for an answer, but she had taken a wet towel and wiped the dust off his body, and afterwards he'd quickly fallen asleep.

This did not stop MaNdlovu worrying, for Ambition seldom slept in the afternoon. Afternoons were a time when he was most active, and outside playing street soccer. He'd also not eaten his morning porridge, so when he woke up MaNdlovu had given him some *isitshwala* and *mopane* worms which she'd prepared for lunch. But much to her further alarm, he'd been sick immediately, and then gone straight back to sleep.

MaNdlovu felt she needed somebody to share the burden of worry, which was beginning to overwhelm her. Her husband had still not returned, after leaving to look for Ambition in the morning. They'd both worried that maybe the child had been caught by the Green Bombers. Then Ngwenya had not returned, and Ntando whom she'd sent to look for him told her that the shopping centre was closed and all the vendors' stalls were deserted. So MaNdlovu called in her neighbour, Ma-Chivanda.

Observing the sleeping child, MaChivanda had offered to give a prayer, and MaNdlovu had, for once, readily agreed. Placing a hand on Ambition's forehead, MaChivanda had prayed loudly and in tongues. Then she'd declared that the bad wind affecting Ambition had been conquered, which had lifted MaNdlovu's worried spirits.

Then MaChivanda had offered to get rid of the pieces of cloth that MaNdlovu had stripped from Ambition, saying they should be thrown away, but MaNdlovu had politely refused. She'd explained that her husband had to see them, so they could decide what to do with them as a family, because this was not a matter to be taken lightly. There seemed, she said, something very bizarre behind it. MaChivanda had not responded, keeping her face blank.

MaNdlovu had noticed that MaChivanda's eyes were also bloodshot and red-rimmed and she also kept coughing and sniffing. 'Just a touch of flu, Auntie. You know when people come to exchange their forex, counting all these new million dollar notes with their new ink affects one. But I'm sure by morning it'll be gone, I have a strong body that recovers quickly.'

MaChivanda had offered another short prayer, this time in Ndebele, thanking uNkulunkulu for taking care of Ambition and the rest of the children in the world, after which she left, saying her forex customers would be waiting for her.

Having escorted her to the gate, MaNdlovu closed the door of the house, took out a salt shaker and sprinkled salt around the sleeping Ambition, while muttering in a low voice, 'Please protect us, Oh spirits of Ngwenya. Our daughter is gone and the same thing must not befall our son. We are all your children, and in your benevolence we trust.'

As she walks slowly down Sibambene Street, MaNdlovu reflects on all the bad luck that has befallen the family. Ambition feels heavy on her back. She will turn into Lotshe Street, where Mr Nkani has his house, and then make her way to Hloniphani Street. She suddenly feels that no matter how fast she walks, she will never arrive. She looks down at her feet clad in *amapatapata* sandals, and takes a deep breath. A grey police truck has turned into the street, and it heads towards her. A tower light rears into the sky as if, like the waning sun, it too is curious about something.

Without hesitating, MaNdlovu turns to her right, opens a gate and walks towards a house with a bright orange door. It's Bra Ngeja's yard. He's a man notorious for being in and out of jail for petty crimes, and has a foul tongue.

MaNdlovu looks behind her. The police truck drives slowly past, ominously loaded with riot police and their perspex shields, helmets, truncheons. MaNdlovu feels trapped. Stepping lightly, not wanting to alert Bra Ngeja, she walks back to the gate, but hears the sound of a door opening behind her.

'What the hell are you doing in my yard?'

Bra Ngeja, carrying a can of Coca Cola and dressed in a white suit, is standing at his door. 'Nothing,' she answers the arrogant young man.

'But you're in my yard, Mama! If you're in love with Bra Ngeja, stop being shy and tell me. You're still nice-looking despite your age and that child on your back.'

MaNdlovu clicks her tongue with disgust. The police truck is well past, and she slips into the road again.

Bra Ngeja laughs contemptuously. '*Viva* ZANU-PF,' his voice follows her. 'Everything you own is ours.'

'Thief!' Ambition calls out, startling his mother who thought he was asleep. 'I bet you stole that Coca-Cola you're drinking!'

'Shut up!' Bra Ngeja points a finger at them. 'I'll get you one day. No one insults me!'

'Shush, Ambition. Please don't create a scene.'

'But he insulted you, Mama.'

'Even if he did, you don't have to insult him back. He's not worth it.'

***

MaNdlovu hums a tune under her breath. It helps to clear her mind. The day has been too full of unpleasant incidents – at least Ambition's sudden show of spirit suggests he is not very ill. A moment later, as she turns into Lotshe Street, her heart jumps.

18

A house is on fire. A crowd of people are scrambling about with buckets, and tossing the water into the building through an open window at the front. A cloud of smoke pours through a back window. A woman is screaming and rolling on the ground beside the gate. A couple of other women keep trying to still her, but each time she manages to break free from their hands.

Suddenly, the woman stops rolling, sits up, stares wildly at MaNdlovu and points a finger at her. 'Witch! You witch! You have come to gloat over the work of your child, have you?'

It is Mrs Nkani.

In the twenty-four years that MaNdlovu has been living in the city, she's never seen a house on fire before. She's only once seen a building burning and that was at the ranch where she and her husband once worked before Independence.

'I saw your daughter do it with my own eyes!' Mrs Nkani screams. 'She threw a petrol bomb into my sitting room. It's you who sent her to do it.'

'Dear God!' MaNdlovu is aghast and begins to sob. 'Dear God!' Ambition slides off her back looking bewildered. 'I swear my family did not send her to do that, Mrs Nkani. It's that terrible militia that she's joined.'

'You made her join it!'

As MaNdlovu is trying to digest these accusations, Mr Nkani races around the corner of the house, a cluster of people following him. He's carrying a bucket that is splashing water over his legs. He stands at the open window, heaves the water in, and rushes away again.

'We did not make her join, Mrs Nkani. She ran away from home. She won't come back.'

'But that's how you made her join,' the teacher's wife says accusingly. 'She ran away from home because you're bad parents!'

'That's not fair, Mrs Nkani.'

'And do you think it's fair that our house is set on fire?'

Before MaNdlovu can reply, a fire engine turns into the street and races towards them, its siren wailing and roof lights flashing.

'You shall pay when the time comes,' Mrs Nkani shouts. 'Go away, I don't want to see you near me!'

MaNdlovu crouches down and Ambition climbs on her back again. Then she walks slowly away, her step heavy. She sniffles as she feels Ambition's hands tighten around her shoulders and his face press against the small of her back.

It's almost dark as MaNdlovu turns into Hloniphani Street and comes to a stop before a closed gate in a stone wall. She places Ambition on his feet. His white T-shirt has 'I ❤ BULAWAYO', on the front. MaNdlovu presses the button on the wall.

'Who is it?' the intercom squawks.

MaNdlovu announces herself, and the electrified gate slowly slides open.

The *inyanga* sits on a brown leather chair in the carpeted sitting room. Two other men sit on sofas.

'Auntie,' the *inyanga* greets MaNdlovu, who's kneeling before him. He points a short ceremonial knobkerrie at Ambition, who's standing slightly behind his mother. 'I see you've brought our father for a visit. What are you saying, Baba?' He smiles at Ambition. Although he's holding a cere-monial staff, the *inyanga* is smartly dressed in a white shirt, grey suit, and matching grey tie.

'Nothing.' There's a shiver to Ambition's voice. He's scared of what the *inyanga* will do to him in the application of the healing for which his mother has carried him all this way.

'Good, my boy, good,' he looks at MaNdlovu and points at an empty sofa. 'Please have a seat, MaNdlovu.'

Now seated, the woman exchanges greetings with the other men in the room, whom she has not seen before.

'You know what, MaNdlovu?' The knobkerrie twirls in the *inyanga*'s hand, and he flashes her a charming smile. 'In the city, medical doctors have working hours in their surgeries, and so do I, here in the township, in my surgery, even if I am a traditional healer.' He laughs briefly. 'I don't work after hours, the ancestors don't allow it.'

Looking at the way the *inyanga* is dressed and at the expensive leather couches, one would not have thought that he was a traditional healer, but a successful modern doctor with a surgery in the city centre.

'My apologies, Baba Gumede, but I could not sleep without seeing you. My husband is not at home right now, otherwise we would have come together and he would have explained the emergency.' MaNdlovu runs a hand down Ambition's back.

'Are you not afraid of the ogres in the streets today, MaNdlovu?'

'My child is not well, Baba. As you can see, his health is more important to me than what is happening in the township.'

'Fair and fine. That's being a good mother. But as I've told you, come with your husband tomorrow. Then you shall receive all the assistance you want. Now the surgery is closed.' He smiles at her again. '*Hamba kahle Mama.*'

Disappointment washes over MaNdlovu, but she does not let it show on her face.

It's been a terrible day.

Chapter 6

When MaNdlovu and Ambition return home, night has descended. The house is as empty as it was when they left. 'Where can your father possibly be?' MaNdlovu asks in a worried voice once they're in the kitchen.

Ambition had felt suddenly frightened when his mother had led him into the *inyanga*'s house. The last time his parents had taken him there was when he'd had a painful rash. The *inyanga*, using a razor blade, had made tiny cuts under both of his tits into which he had smeared *muti*; it had burnt so much he'd cried. So, he'd felt very relieved when the *inyanga* had dismissed them this evening, and had walked all the way home. He seemed to have miraculously recovered. He dreaded another visit, when his father would be with them.

'I can go and look for him at the shops,' he offered. MaNdlovu opens the cupboard and takes out a bag of *mopane* worms and a pot. She pours the worms into the pot, adds water, and places the pot on the stove. Switching the stove on, she goes to the bedroom. Her voice drifts into the kitchen through the curtain that covers the doorway.

'We're now eating *mopane* worms every day, just like the birds. Sometimes I even dream I'm a moth.' Her voice rises. 'Do you know that *mopane* worms turn into moths, Ambition?'

'I didn't know, Mama.'

'What don't you know... Oh these rats, they've made a hole in my burial society skirt!'

'I didn't know that the worms become butterflies when they grow up, Mama. Our teacher has never taught us that.'

'Not butterflies, *moths!* I bet you don't even know the difference. No wonder the teacher's house was burnt. Instead of concentrating on giving you a good education, your teachers are now involved in politics and other dangerous things. This is exactly what your father is always complaining about.'

'Mrs Gumbo is not in politics like Mr Nkani, Mother.'

'It doesn't matter, Ambi. Teachers are the same everywhere. If they're not doing it in public they're doing it in secret.'

The thought of Mrs Gumbo being chased by the Green Bombers flicks through Ambition's mind and he smiles. He wonders if she would out-race them, or even drive them back, just as she had done to Mr Nkani.

'And now they're blaming your sister.' MaNdlovu goes on. 'Throw stones, yes I know Senzeni is capable of doing that, just like many youths of her age. But burn somebody's house – ah no! It's like killing a person. Do you think Senzeni would do that, Ambition?'

'Not Senzeni, Mama, but the Green Bombers. They can beat a person they don't like very hard.'

Ambition is still thinking about Mrs Gumbo. He wishes the year would end quickly, so that he can move to another grade with a new teacher, one who doesn't beat children.

'I wish somebody would catch Senzeni and beat her so hard that she leaves that group,' his mother is saying. 'What does she want from the militia that she cannot get from her home and her parents who pray for her every day?'

'I've never heard you pray, Mama.'

'I pray every day my son, but I don't do it aloud or in tongues or wear a white gown, because I don't want or need to impress anybody.'

***

Ambition remembers that one day he'd been sitting beside his mother under the mulberry tree, trying to do his homework, a composition in Ndebele starting with *Ngelinye ilanga* ... His mother was tying *tshomoliya* leaves into bundles, and placing them in a dish of water. Later she would hawk them around the streets. Suddenly, they heard a voice which Ambition recognised as that of Mr Nkani.

'*Qoki!*'

'It's Mr Nkani, Mama.' MaNdlovu raised her eyebrows with an ex-pression 'Oh is that so?' and called out, 'We're behind the house!' while fastening the top button of her blouse.

Mr Nkani appeared, dressed in jeans and a T-shirt.

'Oh it's Mr Nkani,' his mother feigned surprise, and turned to Ambi-tion. 'Please bring the teacher something to sit on, Ambi.'

23

'You grow taller every day, Ambition,' Mr Nkani smiled as he sat down. 'Just look at you, boy!'

He turned to MaNdlovu, a smile on his rather shy face. 'We're going to have a fine gentleman here. I hear from his teacher that he's doing well in class.'

Ambition wondered why Mrs Gumbo would have told Mr Nkani this. It did not seem that they were friends.

'Thank you, Mr Nkani,' his mother beamed. 'I tell you this one is going to be a doctor. He likes studying. Just look at him.'

'How I wish all my students were like him, Mrs Ngwenya. Studying is very important. We teachers cannot teach everything; some things the students have to discover for themselves – and that's where homework comes in.'

'Certainly, Mr Nkani. But some of our children do not realise this.' Ambition guessed that the conversation was heading towards Senzeni, who'd quickly eaten her lunch, and then had left saying she was going back to school with her friend Mavis for netball practise.

'Our children need to realise that there won't be any parents to turn to once they're adults.' Mr Nkani had continued to edge towards the difficult topic. 'The world we're living in is not so kind, and a good education makes things a bit easier.'

'Are you listening, Ambition?' Ambition had been half-listening and half trying to think about his composition. Mr Nkani was smiling at him.

'Please don't eat your pen, Ambition,' his mother said. 'A pen is food for the hand and the mind, not the mouth. Are you through with your homework?'

'Let me see what you're writing, boy,' Mr Nkani asked before Ambition could reply to his mother.

'*One day when we were playing in the bush with my friend Ntando,*' Mr Nkani read aloud, '*We saw a bird in a nest in a tree, and we climbed up the tree...*'

'Ambi, how many times have I told you never to climb trees? Don't you know it's a very dangerous thing to do?'

'This is only a story MaNdlovu, maybe he was never there at all.'

'Please tell us Ambi, did you climb the tree?'

Ambition thought it wisest not to reply.

'You see,' his mother continued. 'He's so honest he can't even tell a little lie.' She stroked her son's shoulders.

'*We climbed up the tree to the nest,*' Mr Nkani continued, '*Inside the nest were two little babies...*' He laughed. 'We don't say "babies", Ambition.'

'But never mind.' Mr Nkani handed Ambition his exercise book. 'I'll leave you to find out what the babies of birds are called. But you have good imagination, and that's a good start. And your handwriting is good, too.'

'Say thank you to your teacher, Ambition.'

'Thank you, Mr Nkani.'

'No problem, my child. Now where is Senzeni?'

'She's gone back to school to play netball,' Ambition answered quickly.

'Oh, I'd forgotten,' Mr Nkani said to MaNdlovu. 'She's in the netball team and they have a match next week. But it's her class work that has prompted me to visit you today, MaNdlovu.'

'Yes, Mr Nkani, we thank you for coming.' Ambition's mother replied formally to hide her anxiety.

'Senzeni is not doing very well in her class work.'

'That's a difficult matter, Mr Nkani. She's not done well since she started Grade One. We don't even know what to do about it, for we're not educated. Both Ngwenya and I went only up to Form Two. We grew up in the rural areas during the war, and there were so many things disturbing people from education then – and even now.'

'I quite understand you, MaNdlovu. But does Senzeni have time to study at home? Sometimes she doesn't do her homework.'

'That one does not sit down, Mr Nkani, unlike her brother. When she comes from school she takes off her school uniform and as soon as she's had lunch, off she goes again to visit friends.'

'I think you need to be a bit more firm with her. Look at me, MaNdlovu. I'm not shy to say this. My two boys are both at university right now; they were not such bright students, but I made sure that they worked very hard.'

'I know, Mr Nkani. We've tried very hard with Senzeni, but you can't tell her anything. Her father and me have nearly given up.'

'Please don't do so. Just be patient with her. Please keep trying, MaNdlovu, and we at school will do the same. It's not easy raising a child, but we mustn't throw up our hands too early.'

'Thank you, Mr Nkani. I will tell Ngwenya you were here, and what you've advised.'

'I thank you, too,' his face suddenly breaking into a bright smile. 'I see you are getting ready to go and work.'

MaNdlovu laughed. 'People have to eat fresh vegetables Mr Nkani, and I provide them – that is, if they have the money to buy.'

Mr Nkani took a brown wallet from his trouser pocket.

'That is correct, MaNdlovu. So can I please have three bundles? Mrs Nkani bought cow tripe today from the butchery, and I like that with *tshomoliya.*'

Chapter 7

MaNdlovu emerges from the bedroom. She's carrying the reed mat she is working on. She sits on the bench by the stove and starts weaving it on her lap. The shadow of her body falls on the mat from the roof light, seeming to be part of its pattern. The aroma of boiling *mopane* worms fills the room.

'I hate *mopane* worms,' Ambition says, leafing backwards through the torn magazine. 'And I'm not going to eat them. You said they were butterflies, Mama.'

'I did not say they were butterflies, Ambi, but that the worms hatch into moths – what do you hear with?'

'Still I don't like them.'

'Ambi, please, you have to eat so that you can grow up into a strong and intelligent man.' MaNdlovu stands up, opens the cupboard, and takes out a Sun Jam tin. She peers inside it, then spoons out some yellow animal fat and dumps it into the pot.

When the *isitshwala* and *mopane* worms are ready, she forces her sulky son to eat his share, which he does sitting on the floor, with his plate on his lap, while MaNdlovu watches over him.

When Ambition has finished, MaNdlovu has her meal, which she doesn't enjoy either, though in order not to show it, she keeps talking. 'During the Christmas holidays I will ask your father to take you to Nkayi to see your grandparents, my child.' She knows that this is an empty promise, given the scant resources that she and her husband possess, but she feels she has to say something, for she has just discovered that she's afraid. Her husband's absence has left a big hole in the house. She's afraid of the silence that seems to lurk in the shadows of the room.

'I don't want to go.' Ambition lies on the floor, his knees drawn up.

'You don't want to see your grandmother and grandfather?'

'Of course, I do, but I don't want to go to the rural areas.'

'Why ever...?'

'There are no toilets!'

'Where do you think people relieve themselves then?'

'I don't know.'

MaNdlovu can't help laughing.

'So you don't want to squat behind a bush? Remember, some of us grew up in the rural areas doing that every day. Besides, most homes in the rural areas now have Blair toilets.'

'Why are they called "Blair toilets"?'

'I've no idea. Perhaps because the English prime minister is called Tony Blair.'

But Ambition has lost interest.

***

That night, MaNdlovu prepares Ambition's bedding on the bedroom floor beside her own bed, rather than have him sleeping alone in the kitchen. Then she sits down to await her husband's return, keeping her fingers busy with her mat. Sleep will not come to her as long as he stays away.

A little while later she heats a pot of water on the stove and washes herself in the outside toilet; she then heats another pot of water for her husband. Which direction had he taken when he'd gone to look for Ambition all those hours ago? Had he walked into the Green Bombers? If so, could he be lying wounded somewhere? Would Senzeni abandon him to his fate?

Last year, Ngwenya had caught his daughter selling cigarettes in the beer garden, no place and no activity for children of any self-respecting family. Not long afterwards, Senzeni had thrashed MaVundla's son, Power. Then, just a few weeks later, she'd beaten up a girl at her school.

On both occasions, Ngwenya had taken the stick to Senzeni, beating her so hard that even MaNdlovu and Ambition had shed tears. Ngwenya had said that he didn't want to know if Senzeni had been right or wrong, he just didn't want a child who misbehaved. And then, one day, towards the end of the year, Senzeni just dropped out of school.

They'd not realised at first that she was no longer attending her classes because every morning she would dress in her uniform and leave home, apparently for school. It was only when the school orderly had brought a note asking Ngwenya to come to the school to see the headmaster that they'd found out.

Ngwenya had been very angry and had confronted his daughter as soon as she came home.

'Where have you been, Senzeni? We know you've not been to school.' Senzeni stared into her lap.

'Please, answer your father, Senzeni,' MaNgwenya had cajoled her daughter, pain in her heart. She just didn't know what, if anything, was wrong with Senzeni. She just wanted her to finish her Form Four like other children, even if she only got bad marks.

'Do you want me to take out my stick?' Ngwenya had threatened. Senzeni did not reply.

'Am I going to get an answer from you?' Ngwenya was breathing heavily, his anger barely under control.

'I don't want to go to school anymore,' Senzeni finally answered in a small voice.

'Senzeni, you can't say that!' MaNdlovu had been the first to speak.

'I don't want school anymore,' Senzeni repeated very quietly.

'But why?' Ngwenya's voice was resigned rather than angry. 'What's wrong with school?'

'I don't like it,' was all she would say.

Ngwenya had not taken the stick to Senzeni, as everybody had expected. Instead, he'd left home and gone to the beer garden.

***

A few months later, MaNdlovu's petticoat disappeared from the wardrobe.

MaNdlovu's fingers hang for a moment over the mat. She wishes she'd not remembered, it had been so shameful, and because of it her daughter had ended up joining the Green Bombers.

It had been a Monday that she realised her new petticoat was missing. She'd bought it from MaVundla, who bought women's clothing and toiletries in Botswana for sale in the township. It was the same morning that Ambition had said there was going to be a school trip to the Matopo Hills, and that it cost Z$10,000. She'd had to say no because the rent and electricity were in arrears.

'It's okay, Mama. I will go some other time, it's not important.' That he took the disappointment so well, somehow made MaNdlovu feel worse and she'd sighed as she looked at Senzeni, who was scrubbing the kitchen floor.

Just a few seconds later, MaVundla had appeared at the door.

'Hello, my customer,' she'd greeted MaNdlovu, in her special sales voice. She was carrying a bright red bag full of women's underwear.

'These are special, Thenjiwe!' There was a naughty glint in her eyes. 'I tell you, when Samson...' she referred to Ngwenya by his first name '... sees you in these ...' she held up a pair of red satin panties, '... your love for each other will be as it was when you met.'

MaNdlovu was embarrassed, and she hustled MaVundla outside. 'No, no, I can't afford any new underwear,' her eyes fastened on the open bag of silky garments.

MaVundla was undeterred. 'Okay, buy these two petticoats for the price of one, and I will give you a pair of panties for free.'

MaNdlovu hesitated. How long was it since she'd bought anything for herself? And three for one ... she could give one or the other to Senzeni.

But that same day, when she'd looked for her new petticoat and the panties after she'd had her bath, they were no longer in the drawer in her wardrobe. She'd searched everywhere, and drew a blank. Senzeni was out, so she could not ask her, and it seemed as if Senzeni's new petticoat had also disappeared, unless the girl was wearing it.

1977

Chapter 8

Jiba is a small village to the north of the Plumtree district. From Bulawayo, you take the strip road past Solusi Mission and the cluster of commercial farms known as ko Mekisi. When you reach the crossroads of Ekhoneni, you turn left via Ntunungwe and the Plumtree district. You will pass through the villages of Ntunungwe, Halimane and Tshangwa, before you reach Jiba village and Thenjiwe Ndlovu's home.

Thenjiwe had come home with her two young sisters at sunset, after fetching water at the nearby Natali River. She found her father sitting in the shade of the big *musasa* tree. He was not alone. Mbambo, a neighbour, was with him. He was in his blue overalls and black gum boots, the prestigious uniform of the neighbouring Wildberg Ranch. The stool he sat on was elaborately carved and reserved for important guests.

'Come and greet our visitor after you've put the water in the kitchen,' Ndlovu called out as his daughers came in through the gate and made a beeline for the kitchen door.

Thenjiwe's mother was building a fire in the smoke-filled kitchen. 'Good news for you,' MaKhumalo smiled, as she leant down to blow into the fire.

'I don't want to hear about it,' Thenjiwe replied sullenly, placing her heavy bucket on the floor.

'But it's good for you, Thenjiwe,' MaKhumalo insisted, fanning the fire with a metal plate. 'Many girls in the village are dying for such a chance, my dear daughter.'

'No!' Thenjiwe's jaw clenched.

Sukoluhle and Nomvelo, who had placed their buckets down too, were staring at their sister in concentrated silence. They had discussed this matter many times before in the girls' sleeping hut, and both were on Thenjiwe's side. Once, in her absence, the two girls had taken up the matter with their mother, speaking strongly against their father's wish, but MaKhumalo had silenced them with a strongly veiled threat. 'Your father wants it, and his word is final. So, if it is not your sister, then it will be someone else in this household who knows that Ndlovu is their father and I, MaKhumalo, am their mother.' The words had quickly silenced the two dissenting voices.

'Go and greet our visitor, girls,' MaKhumalo instructed in a soft voice, placing sticks in the growing fire, and then, her voice assumed a mock scolding tone, 'People, please tell me what has happened to the word respect in the Ndlovu household, *shuwa?*'

Her daughters trooped out.

Thenjiwe knelt on the ground before Mbambo and extended a limp right hand to him.

'I see you, *Baba.*' She stressed the word baba, to make him aware that he was much too old to become her husband.

Mbambo had a smooth round face, like the grey pestle her mother used to grind nuts. A thick moustache hung over his upper lip. Thenjiwe knew that he was a few years younger than her father, who was in his fifties, because his first-born son, who had disappeared across the border in the early seventies, heading for the guerrilla camps, had been older than her by a few years.

Mbambo grasped her hand in his. It was tough and dry. 'I see you, MaNdlovu,' he responded. 'How are you, my dear?'

She'd almost grimaced when he had called her that, but of course she couldn't do so in front of her father. She pulled her hand away from his, stood up, and walked swiftly towards the door of the kitchen, which was puffing out a thick cloud of smoke, as if in protest at the meeting under the *musasa* tree.

'Thenjiwe!' Her father's firm voice stopped her. She turned around. Sukoluhle was standing before Mbambo, while Nomvelo knelt before him, though his eyes were fixed on Thenjiwe.

'Baba?'

'Don't go away yet. Come and sit down.' Ndlovu's voice was curt, his brow furrowed. Thenjiwe walked slowly back towards them.

Aged fourteen and twelve, Nomvelo and Sukoluhle had both left school together with Thenjiwe, when their father's cattle had succumbed to drought the previous year. It was their father who'd cut short their education; he insisted that they needed to help their mother in the fields and around home so that the family could eat.

'You can go and help your mother in the kitchen, girls,' Ndlovu instructed his two younger daughters. 'This matter only concerns your sister, Thenjiwe.'

The two girls both looked at their father in dismay as they turned and walked towards the kitchen. Thenjiwe sat down beside her father, her feet folded beneath her. Mbambo grinned and Thenjiwe felt her skin crawl.

'Mbambo has brought some good news for you, my daughter.' Mbambo's grin had widened, revealing teeth stained by cigarettes.

Thenjiwe remained silent, her eyes focused on a long line of ants that were cutting across the ground heading towards the gate, as if they also disapproved of what was about to happen.

'Are you listening, Thenjiwe?' Ndlovu's voice was almost a bark.

'Yes I am, Father,' Thenjiwe replied in a small voice.

'As you see him,' her father pointed a finger at Mbambo, his teeth were still bared in a rusty grin. 'He's going on a long vacation from the ranch, but he's been kind enough to stop by and share with us some very good news from there.'

'Very good *indeed*,' Mbambo echoed.

Thenjiwe scooped a handful of sand and let it trickle slowly between her fingers, while her eyes remained fixed on the line of migrating ants.

'Good news coming from bad news ...' Ndlovu shrugged his shoulders, looking at Mbambo. 'But what can we do about it if their God wishes it to be so?'

'It is beyond our hands,' Mbambo said. Thenjiwe felt lost, not knowing what was being referred to.

Ndlovu's eyes settled on Thenjiwe. There was a glitter in them she recognised from the days when one of his cows had successfully given birth.

'You are now grown up, my dear daughter,' he announced, abruptly switching tracks.

'I am *not*, father! I only turn eighteen next month. I am still seventeen!'

'A person does not see herself if she is grown up or not,' Ndlovu went on. 'Sometimes it takes another eye to do that.' He looked at Mbambo. 'Am I lying, Baba Mbambo?'

'Definitely not. Even I sometimes think of myself as a boy, and it shocks me to hear children refer to me as "that man" when I pass by!'

Ndlovu and Mbambo grinned at each other.

'So you see, Thenjiwe.' Ndlovu's voice was soft and sweet. 'You might think you are still a girl, but some children refer to you as you pass by as "that woman"!' The grins of the two men turned to laughter.

'Okay, now to be serious on a very *serious* occasion,' Ndlovu said, his face grave. Thenjiwe tensed, feeling anger welling out of her heart. He couldn't do this to her. No! She had actually never talked to him about it, but her mother had intimated several times that it was her father's wish that she should marry this man.

'Daughters are there to bring in a dowry,' MaKhumalo had told her three daughters one summer night as they sat together around the embers of a fire after supper. 'And this household is lucky because I gave your father three beautiful women. Just look at you, my dear daughters – wooo, you are the envy of the whole village!'

'But Mama,' Sukoluhle had replied, 'that's not true!'

'Oh, so I did not give birth to any beautiful girls who are now the envy of the village?'

'Sukoluhle doesn't mean that, Mama,' Nomvelo had interjected. 'You know what she means.'

'Don't you know it is taboo in our culture to say your parent is lying?' MaKhumalo had snapped. 'You might wake up with no breasts one morning if you're not careful!'

'I didn't mean it that way, Mother!' Sukoluhle said, her hands brushing her bosom. 'What I'm trying to say is that my teacher at school said that parents do not give birth to their daughters so that they can bring in a dowry, but so that the daughters can live just as anybody and fulfil their own wishes.'

'Oh how educated you've become out of of the generosity of your father,' MaKhumalo said firmly. 'See now, the children are telling their parents what to do, just like white children.'

'You're the youngest, Sukoluhle,' MaKhumalo went on, a snap in her voice, 'and the most stubborn. Aren't you ashamed of yourself? But let me tell you something for nothing. If you continue thinking like this, marriage will never come your way, and which woman in her right senses wishes that on herself?'

Now her father had taken the bold step, Thenjiwe thought, her eyes on the ants which still marched towards the gate. She had an uncanny feeling that she was a cabbage laid out for sale. She wondered if the prospective buyer would pick her up and pinch her to see if she was firm.

'There's been a serious accident at Wildberg Ranch,' Ndlovu said. 'Please tell her, Baba Mbambo.'

Mbambo cleared his throat. 'The son of the owner of Wildberg Ranch was travelling to town with his wife last week when they drove over a landmine,' he announced. 'They were killed on the spot, and they've left behind their four-year-old baby. His name is Tom; he's being looked after by his grandmother, but I've been asked to look for a nanny to help her.'

Ndlovu smiled. 'You helped your mother with your two sisters when they were growing up – I remember you crooning to them whenever they cried. You'll make a good nanny for this child, my daughter.'

'But... ' she stammered, astonished, 'it's a white baby that you're talking about, Father!'

'Black or white, they all fart the same!' Ndlovu snapped. 'Please don't try to complicate a very simple situation. It's your future we are talking about, and you should be grateful.'

'Children are no problem,' Mbambo added. 'You just tie them to your back, rock them a little and sing *thula thula sana* and you've won their hearts.' Thenjiwe sensed a trap, but could not quite put a finger on it, so she decided to change tactics.

'You're going on leave, Mr Mbambo?' she asked innocently, her eyes averted.

'Yes I am,' Mbambo replied, seeming happy to be directly addressed at last. 'I've been working non-stop on the ranch for the past four years. It's time I had a short rest.'

'Will you be staying there during your vacation?' Thenjiwe heard a whirr of wings and a dove started to coo, a peaceful echoic sound that contrasted with her conflicted emotions.

'No, thank you, I will be at my homestead. The vacation is for a three full months.'

'You must also find employment for me, Baba Mbambo,' Ndlovu said, a smile creasing his thin cheeks. 'How many times have I asked you to do so? You're the foreman aren't you?'

'I might be the foreman, Ndlovu, but unfortunately for you, I don't hire. Mr Phillips or his wife does that, and for now we don't need anyone. MaNdlovu is only lucky to get this job because of that unfortunate landmine. But if anything comes up, you'll be the first to know, I promise you.'

'Let it not be because of another landmine,' Ndlovu replied. He turned to Thenjiwe. 'Are we now agreed that you will take the job?'

'Yes, I will take it.'

A smile flitted across Mbambo's face.

Chapter 9

At sunrise the following morning, Thenjiwe had left for Wildberg Ranch. Sukolohle and Nomvelo had escorted her half the way, following a narrow track that ribboned through the countryside. It had been the onset of spring, and the countryside was luminous with the tender green of fresh leaves, and with them a hint of the first rains to follow.

The two younger sisters took turns to help Thenjiwe carry the suitcase that held her few clothes. It was half a day's journey by foot to the ranch, and two hours after they'd started, the three sisters stopped beside a clump of bushes; it was time for Sukoluhle and Nomvelo to turn back home.

'I still feel you shouldn't have agreed to work at the ranch, Thenjiwe,' Sukoluhle said. 'You'll be caught right inside that horrible man's trap.'

'We know he's going on vacation for three months,' Thenjiwe replied, 'and so I have a grace period. When he returns, I'll be careful, and if things are not good, I will come back home. Maybe father will have had second thoughts by then.'

'But are you sure he's on vacation?' Nomvelo asked. 'We don't trust him, and maybe he was lying, and he and father are conspiring against you.'

'I hadn't thought of that, but let me get to the ranch first and see how things stand. I will take it from there. I have no other choice. If I were to run away from home, where would I go?'

'Mbambo is too old for you, Thenjiwe,' Sukoluhle said fiercely, as she gave her sister a goodbye hug. 'You need a handsome young man as a husband.'

'Find one for me, dear Sukoluhle, and I will be the happiest woman in the village.' Hearing a slight rustle, Thenjiwe turned, then grabbed both her sisters by the shoulders and pushed them to the ground.

'Down!'

Instantly, they crouched behind a bush. Sukoluhle and Nomvelo were looking at Thenjiwe, their eyes wide with alarm. The older girl placed a finger across her lips, and pointed. A man appeared from the bushes on the other side of the track. He was dressed in a khaki combat jacket and cap, and carried a rifle. He crossed the track in one stride and was gone, heading north-west.

'ZIPRA,' Nomvelo whispered. The sisters straightened up, and then immediately crouched down again. Another man was crossing the track. He wore rice camouflage and a black beret with large sunglasses covering his eyes. He too was carrying a rifle, and a piece of black cloth was wound around his right wrist.

After a short lull, a group of men appeared, walking in single file. Almost all of them were dressed in half-military, half-civilian clothes. They all carried guns, backpacks, and had bullet belts across their bodies.

The girls waited silently, their hearts beating loudly. At last, Thenjiwe stood up, and her sisters followed suit. 'You'd better hurry home as fast as you can.' She put the suitcase on her head. 'Be careful, won't you?'

'We'll write to you,' her sisters promised.

'And please come and visit us on your off-duty days,' Nomvelo said.

'If I hear of anybody coming your way, I will write too,' Thenjiwe promised. 'And, yes, I promise to visit when I get time.'

Thenjiwe set off. She let her mind float as her feet trod rhythmically along the path. After she had covered a good distance, the track widened, an indication that she was not far from the ranch. It was now midday. A short while later she came to a wooden stile over a barbed-wire fence and climbed over it. She was now within the ranch grounds, but the house wasn't visible; she thought it was about half-an-hour's walk away.

Continuing, she noticed a patch of tall elephant grass to the side of the track, the kind that village women sometimes walked a long way to collect, because it made good thatching and could be used for weaving mats and baskets; although on the ranch they would have to ask for permission first, or risk arrest.

She was startled from her reverie when the elephant grass suddenly swayed; but there was no wind – surely, she thought, not more guerrillas. She was preparing to duck when she heard a loud snort, and a buffalo shot out of the grass and thundered towards her.

Instantly dropping her suitcase, she ran towards a big *marula* tree to her right. Fear lent wings to her heels. She was going to die. That thought was just the catapult she needed. She leapt and her hands found purchase on the rough bark of the lowest branch. Her feet swung forward following the impetus of her body and she heard the buffalo gallop past beneath her. She felt sure the heels of her shoes had brushed against the top of its body.

Clinging to the branch, her arms sore, her hands grazed, her body heavy, she saw the buffalo came to an abrupt stop and turn back towards her. She was almost sure she saw it grin. She would have grinned too if she'd been it, for she was hanging from the branch like washing on a line. The buffalo pawed the ground as if about to charge.

Gathering all her strength and with a powerful twist Thenjiwe swung her body up and on to the branch as the buffalo, now bewildered, charged under the tree. Panting with fear, she suddenly heard dogs barking and a pack of six or seven streaked into sight and raced at the buffalo, which turned and disappeared from view in the tall elephant grass.

A man was running towards the tree when Thenjiwe jumped down. Her feet crumpled beneath her and she fell. She felt strong hands grasp her under the armpits and lift her to her feet. The man was young, and his tough lean face was filled with concern.

'Are you all right?'

Thenjiwe nodded. She felt okay. She could hear the dogs barking in the distance. She took a few deep breaths to steady herself.

'Where are you going?' asked the man, who was dressed in the blue overalls of Wildberg Ranch.

'To the ranch house,' Thenjiwe replied, and suddenly found herself smiling shyly, like a person caught in an embarrassing situation. 'I think that buffalo would have killed me if you hadn't arrived.'

'You're lucky, there are plenty of them around here. White people come to hunt them. But, on the whole, they are not dangerous unless they're frightened.' He paused. 'But you'd best get on now. If you're heading to the ranch house, go that way. I'm going with the dogs.'

Thenjiwe had meant to ask for his family name so as to thank him properly, but he was already gone, running after the dogs.

Slowly, still breathing hard, she went and picked up her suitcase. She hoped today's misadventures were not an omen.

***

She finally reached the ranch house, a large picturesque building with white walls and a red roof surrounded by a high barbed-wire fence. Now she felt a different kind of fear. She had never in her life talked to a white person, but only seen them from a distance and, of course, soldiers sometimes arrived unannounced in the villages – and now she was expected to live with them. A part of her mind was telling her to run back to Jiba village and her home, but her tired feet said otherwise. They took her right up to the tall gate, the suitcase still on her head. The gate was locked. Dogs rushed at her from inside it, all barking furiously.

A white woman with long hair appeared from around the back of the house and walked towards the gate. A small stout dog walked beside her. Thenjiwe breathed heavily as the woman reached the gate. Her heart was beating. The dogs immediately stopped barking and they all fell in behind her, but the stout dog stood at the woman's side, its head raised and re-garding Thenjiwe quizically.

'How can I help you?' The woman addressed Thenjiwe in English. Dressed in khaki pants and blouse, she looked almost as strong as a man.

'I am look for job,' Thenjiwe replied in her halting English, which she'd learned at school.

The woman regarded her for a moment from head to toe before she reached down and stroked the head of her small dog, 'Sorry, no job, *nka-zana*.' Thenjiwe was taken aback. 'No job? Foreman Mbambo say you have baby job for me. He tell my father that.'

'You should have said that straightaway,' the older woman said reproach-fully. 'Baby job, for goodness sake!'

The woman looked at Thenjiwe again and saw a strong young village woman wearing a clean cotton frock and carrying a battered cardboard suitcase. 'What's your name?'

'Thenjiwe.'

'That means one who's trusted,' the woman had said, switching to per-fect Ndebele. 'I don't want a bloody terrorist, I can tell you. You know what happened to my son and daughter-in-law. I'm Mrs Phillips, your new employer. Please come in.' She unlocked and opened the gate.

Chapter 10

Mrs Phillips's husband was away 'doing his stint in this dreadful war,' as the older woman explained, so for the moment she was at home with her grandson, Tom, and the ranch workers.

Looking after Tom had been a challenge. He appeared to throw tantrums for no reason, at least that's how it seemed to Thenjiwe, who often felt helpless before them. It's difficult to comfort a child when neither of you are familiar with the same language.

'It's because he's suddenly lost his parents and his home,' Mrs Phillips told Thenjiwe one afternoon when Tom howled on the veranda. 'He's lost and bewildered.' Then her voice changed from sympathy to anger. 'These ZIPRA terrorists have no heart! Why kill civilians, fathers and mothers? Do they want children to grow up as orphans?'

Thenjiwe thought about the ZIPRA combatants who were also fathers and mothers who were being massacred every day by the Rhodesian Front forces, but she knew it was best to keep quiet.

***

While Mr Phillips was away, Thenjiwe was given a room at the back of the main house. The rest of the staff lived in a compound a short distance away behind it, and a thick bougainvillea separated the two.

But six weeks later, when Mr Phillips returned from the war, his wife allocated Thenjiwe a hut in the compound, and told her: 'When Mr Phillips is away, you sleep in the main house, but when he's around, you sleep in the compound, okay? I don't want any funny business happening in my house behind my back.' Whatever that meant escaped Thenjiwe's comprehension.

When she took up her dwelling in the workers' compound, she was no longer the young woman she'd been when she first arrived at the ranch.

Regular, good food had given a lustre to her skin and her body had filled out. She also had a uniform, a blue dress with tiny white flowers and a white apron, with a matching doek, and brown tennis shoes. So it was no wonder that she became an instant hit amongst the men, some of whom she knew. Proposals flowed in, but Thenjiwe was not such an easy young woman.

And so the girl settled into her new life, and slowly Tom became easier to manage, and Thenjiwe's English improved. One afternoon, several weeks later, after she'd helped Mrs Phillips clean out a cupboard, she was given a pair of shoes with worn heels. 'If you take them to Samson in the compound, he'll fix them for you and I'm sure you'll be able use them for some time to come,' Mrs Phillips said.

Thenjiwe had never met the cobbler, although she'd heard that there was a ranch hand who mended shoes in his spare time. So, over the weekend, she'd found him sitting in the shade of a tree working on a recalcitrant heel, a pile of shoes beside him.

'Sabona,' Thenjiwe greeted him as he looked up. It was the young man she'd met when she'd been trying to escape the buffalo.

'*Yebo, kunjani?*' the man smiled at her.

'I didn't know you were the cobbler,' Thenjiwe found herself saying. 'Do you remember me?' The man looked at her closely. 'You don't?' Thenjiwe smiled.

'I'm sorry, no. You work in the main house don't you?'

'I'm the new maid there,' Thenjiwe answered, 'but I'm also the one that jumped from the tree after your dogs had chased that buffalo away.'

The man laughed. 'Oh yes, I remember. That was funny.'

'Yes it's funny now but I was very scared at the time. If I hadn't been, I don't think I could have leapt up into that tree.'

'When we're very frightened we can do the impossible.'

'Did your dogs catch the buffalo?'

'No, no, it wasn't our intention to catch it, but to just scare it away. It was a loner, and had got too close to the house, frightening people. If the dogs had caught and killed it, I'd be out of a job.'

'But what if it had killed me?'

The man laughed again. 'You don't matter. You don't bring forex into the country as the white trophy hunters do.'

'What's forex?'

'Money from overseas. It's very valuable to your employer; you must

42

know that since you work in the main house so close to them.'

'Mmh, I've never seen it,' said Thenjiwe. 'But thanks again. I'm sure you saved my life. I meant to find you and ask for your surname so that I could thank you properly, but never did and now we meet again by chance.'

'I am Samson Ngwenya.'

'And I am Thenjiwe Ndlovu.'

She knelt on one knee and extended her right hand. Ngwenya wiped his own on the trouser of his overalls, and gripped hers.

'Thank you so much, Baba Ngwenya, and may the spirits of my forefathers look after your shadow till you reach a ripe old age.'

'Thank you MaNdlovu, and may you grow up and give the world many strong children.'

They shook hands.

***

Working in the main house offered Thenjiwe a protected life that some of the ranch workers in the compound would have given an arm for, as she lived almost like the family for whom she was working. But it had its drawbacks. She sometimes found herself longing for the company and conversations of people in her own village, people she could talk to as equals.

Although she had stayed in her room in the compound several times and for several weeks, she had not yet found anyone that she could socialise with, as she arrived late in the evening, and left very early in the morning to return to the main house.

'And now what can I do for you?' Samson asked after they'd shaken hands.

'I have heels that need fixing, Ngwenya.' She took her shoes from the plastic bag and showed them to him.

He inspected the heels. 'These are very good shoes,' he said. 'And yes, I can fix the heels.' He placed the shoes on the pile in front of him. 'You can come back for them tomorrow.' Samson picked up the shoe he'd been working on.

At that moment, they heard a faint roar in the sky. Samson looked up, needle in hand, as two low-flying helicopters in army colours flew overhead in the direction of the village.

'Trouble for the brothers,' Samson said as they watched the helicopters disappear over the treetops.

'Please call me Samson – I'm not that old.'

'Okay, Samson,' Thenjiwe smiled. 'When I first came here about two months ago I met a group of them.'

'Who?'

'The brothers.' She told him about the guerrillas she'd seen with her two sisters whom they'd assumed were ZIPRA forces.

'One of them wore large dark sunglasses and had a black cloth tied around his wrist.' She described the man who'd stood out from the rest of the group.

'They don't sound familiar,' Samson replied. 'Must be a new group in the area.'

'I hope the helicopters won't find them.'

Samson looked at her thoughtfully as he started working on the shoe again.

Chapter 11

In 1977 the war of liberation was escalating. Firefights between the Rhodesian army and the defiant guerrillas became a regular feature of life in rural Zimbabwe. At sunset that same day, as Thenjiwe cooked her supper on the fire behind her hut, she heard the protracted sound of gunfire and explosions, and she prayed that her family were safe in the village.

But the following day was peaceful, and dressed in her best blue dress she went to collect her shoes from Samson. To her surprise, she found Mbambo sitting on a bench beside the cobbler. A dirty bandage was tied round his head. He was wearing one boot, while Samson worked on a tear on the side of the other. A shotgun rested against Mbambo's knee.

Thenjiwe decided to walk past the cobbler, wanting to avoid Mbambo, but Samson called out, 'Your shoe is finished, MaNdlovu.' Slowly she turned round. Mbambo's openly admiring eyes were fixed on her. She saw her shoes on the pile next to Samson, and she picked them up and studied them. Both heels had been repaired, and they looked as good as new.

'How much?' she asked, wondering to herself if she had brought enough money.

'Greet the ranch foreman first, daughter of Ndlovu,' Mbambo said in a reproachful voice.

Thenjiwe greeted him politely, curtsying a little. 'Is the vacation over so soon, Baba Mbambo?'

'Yes it is.'

'I thought you said you'd be away for three months...'

'Well, you heard wrong.' His voice was curt. 'I said two months, and I came back last night.'

'I heard you clearly, and you said three!' Thenjiwe said stubbornly.

Samson looked up, sensing antipathy.

'Let's not argue,' Mbambo responded. 'It's not my problem if your beautiful ears didn't hear correctly.' He smiled at her lasciviously and a shudder ran down Thenjiwe's spine.

'How much do I owe you?' she asked Samson.

'How much do you want to give me?'

'The bill is on me, Samson,' Mbambo said.

'Oh no, I'm paying, I must pay!' Thenjiwe reached into her pocket where she kept her money.

'Let's not argue,' Mbambo said. 'Samson, let her take the shoes.'

'Sure, Baba Mbambo,' he smiled. 'But you didn't bring the shoes to me.'

Mbambo's face swelled with anger. 'Will you please repeat that?'

'I mean, this is not ranch business, and I'm the boss in this shoe shop.'

'I said give the woman her shoes, dammit!'

'My money, boss?'

'Do you think I can't afford to pay you such little money, Samson? And yet I found you employment here and had you made assistant foreman!'

'A tickey, boss.' Samson was not giving any ground.

Mbambo scowled, and took a handful of coins from his pocket. He selected a tickey and held it out to Samson. 'Fool!'

'Thanks boss,' Samson said, taking the coin. 'Being a businessman is so troublesome if one is not careful with one's employers.'

Mbambo clicked his tongue in disgust.

'Thank you, Baba Mbambo,' Thenjiwe said, not wanting any more arguments.

Mbambo took an envelope from his overall pocket.

'This is from your father,' he said. 'I saw him yesterday on my way here.'

Thenjiwe took the letter, looked at Samson who was bent over Mbambo's boot, and turned to walk away.

'Not even a thank you?' Mbambo's voice followed her.

'Thank you for delivering the letter, Baba Mbambo.' Thenjiwe tossed the words over her shoulder.

'Your father said you must give me the reply as soon as you've read it. I'm going back to the village tomorrow morning and I will be seeing him.'

***

Thenjiwe read the letter as soon as she reached her room. It was not from her father, but from the man who thought she was a sitting duck.

My Sweet Water Melon

You are so delicious to look at that every time I think of you I want to wear my new cowboy hat from South Africa, and with it on my head, I will come to your hut to tell you that your true home is in the ranch palace, which is my cottage in the compound. There everything will be at your fingertips, and all the other ranch workers will come to kiss your toes for you will be their Queen. Let me not hide it from you that your father is my dearest friend, and I sympathise with his loss of his cattle because of this drought. But please rest assured that your father's misery will soon be over, because I have more than eighty head of cattle and I am prepared to give him fifteen as your dowry. Isn't that a lot of cows for him?

Your husband to be.

Thunder Mbambo

Thenjiwe crumpled the letter in her hand and flung it away. The ball of scrunched paper hit the wall and bounced to the floor. She felt like screaming with anger and frustration.

She walked out of the compound and followed a path that led out of the ranch, making a huge effort effort not to think of Mbambo. If this is what it meant to become a woman, there was no pleasure in it. She would rather she'd remained a child. How could her parents, who had once loved her, force her into a marriage with such a toad!

It was a hot day, and the countryside lay still around her, as if waiting for sunset. Her eyes were alert to any movement but nothing moved, except for the flutter of an occasional bird.

Did her parents hate her? Were they trying to get rid of her by offering her to Mbambo? She'd never done them any wrong as far as she could remember. She had done all her household chores diligently; she was respectful and showed her love for her parents and her sisters whenever she could. Did wealth matter so much? Were her parents so poor that they had to sell her? It was a chilling thought.

What if she walked all the way to her home right now? She might avoid Mbambo this way, but if her father was determined that she marry him, her relief would be short-lived. Would her parents lock her up, and send for Mbambo to come and get her as if she were a goat?

She found herself muttering, 'Don't agree, never agree. Your life is your own, don't give in'. Once she had leapt into a tree to escape a buffalo. The will to survive had given her strength. Could she summon up more strength to escape this latest hazard? Thenjiwe knew she had to find a way to do so. She turned round and slowly made her way back to the ranch, her mind determined.

Chapter 12

By the time she reached the compound, the sun had set but it was not yet dark. Thenjiwe prepared herself a supper of *isitshwala* and dried fish. She ate by the fireside, watching the stars in the sky, attempting to discharge the last traces of anger in her heart.

After eating, she washed her utensils, doused the coals and went back inside. There, she lit a candle, and picked up Mbambo's crumpled letter. Straightening it out, she re-read it. After a few minutes, she clapped her hands in a gesture of amazement, before thrusting the letter into the candle flame. Once it was reduced to ash, she took a grass broom, and with careful strokes, swept the ash towards the door. Just then, above the swish of the broom, she heard a noise and then a sudden knock. Nobody ever visited her hut after sunset.

'Who is it?'

'A visitor.' She instantly recognised Mbambo's voice.

She let the broom drop from her hand and stood for a moment, her heart beating.

The knock came again. She took a deep breath, and opened the door.

Mbambo stood outside. He was dressed in a dark suit, and a white cowboy hat on his head, the two sides of its brim seeming like horns. A scent emanated from him that she recognised as mothballs. Behind Mbambo, the moon had risen, and sat in passive silence.

'Good evening, Mr Mbambo,' she greeted him in an expressionless voice.

'Visitors are supposed to be invited inside the house before they're greeted,' Mbambo responded. His right hand was inside the pocket of his jacket. 'That is what we're taught when we're growing up in homes with respected names, MaNdlovu, and especially a home like your father's.'

'It's late,' she replied. 'I'm now preparing for bed.'

'It might be late for others to visit you, but not too late for some.' His teeth flashed. He removed his hand from his jacket pocket and held out an orange.

'I've brought this sweet fruit for a sweet lady,' he announced.

'I don't eat fruit,' Thenjiwe replied quickly. 'Especially oranges!'

'Well, well, what a surprise.' Mbambo gave her a sideways look. 'This is my first time to meet someone who does not eat oranges. Maybe the food you eat in the ranch kitchen is sweeter than the food you had in the village before I got you this job?'

Thenjiwe sniffed, and made to push the door closed with her hand, but Mbambo placed his hand on the doorknob. 'Not yet,' he said. Thenjiwe could feel the man's lustful eyes on her. 'What has happened to the manners that I've always admired in all the daughters of Ndlovu – especially you, Thenjiwe?'

'It is late and I want to sleep. Tomorrow is Sunday. I have to get up early to go to work.'

'If there's still work for you... ' Mbambo let the threat hang in the air. Then propping the door ajar with his foot, he leant down and placed the orange on the doorstep. Dogs began to bark somewhere in the compound and suddenly Thenjiwe recalled the image of the pack racing towards the buffalo. How she wished Samson would appear now with his dogs and chase Mbambo away.

'Or maybe I should have done this in the first place,' Mbambo said, straightening up. 'Enjoy the orange. I expect to find its peel outside your door tomorrow morning as a sign that you've agreed to my proposal of marriage. Good night.' He released the door and walked away.

Chapter 13

Thenjiwe stood watching Mbambo's back as he disappeared into the moonlight. Then she looked at the orange. It sat on the doorstep, as if taunting her. She drew her right foot back, poised for a hard kick, but hesitated, and put her foot down. But she could not control the impulse, and instead picked up the orange and hurled it into the night.

'Ouch!' She heard an angry cry. 'Who's hit me?'

The young woman gave a startled gasp. Samson stepped out of the darkness into the moonlight, one hand covering his eye.

'Did you see who threw this?' he asked her crossly. 'Can't a man take a simple walk without being hurt?'

Thenjiwe stepped forward.

'I'm so sorry!' She stepped nearer. 'Can I please have a look?' She gently removed his hand and tilted his head to the moonlight. Unbidden, she could feel a smile rising from deep within her, but she kept her face impassive.

'It's not swollen,' she said. 'Please wait here a moment.'

She turned back into her room, returning a moment later with a damp towel. She pressed it to his eye, slowly counting one to ten. Then she removed the towel and looked at the eye again.

'I think it's going to be all right.'

'Thank you,' he said. 'Fancy people throwing away something so delicious ... or were they trying a prank on the ranch cobbler?' He began peeling the orange. 'Maybe someone is not happy that I make a little side money mending shoes.'

'I'm sure it's not that.'

'But why?' Samson chuckled. 'How can I be hit by a flying orange in the middle of the night? It's very odd. Funny really, since I'm not injured.'

Thenjiwe wondered if he knew the story behind the orange; maybe he'd been watching from the darkness, and was only teasing her. She decided not to say anything, but smiled.

'And since this fruit caused me pain,' Samson continued, 'I'm going to cause it pain. I'm going to eat it.'

'Oh no, please don't!'

'Why shouldn't I? Just give me one good reason and I'll spare its orange life.'

A radio was suddenly turned on and rock and roll music blared out across the compound.

'Do you know where the orange came from?'

'That's the least of my worries,' the cobbler announced. 'To me an orange is an orange, and it only comes from one place, an orange tree. But...' He paused. 'There are so many trees growing in the orchard behind Mbambo's house; do you think he might have thrown it? After all, he's also the one making all that noise with his radio right now.'

'I don't think Mbambo threw it.' Thenjiwe felt this was the strangest evening of all her life.

She tried to change the subject. 'Do you have any children?'

'What if I have?'

'Then you could give them the orange.'

'Well, I don't have any. I just have dogs, and they don't eat oranges, so I've no one to share the fruit with ...' Samson's eyes twinkled. 'Can I share it with you, MaGatsheni?' He neatly twisted the fruit so it split in half, and held out some segments to Thenjiwe.

A warm feeling settled on Thenjwe's heart when Solomon called her by her totem, but she took a step backwards, as if shying away.

'I don't want it, Sitshela.' She responded with his totem.

'You don't eat oranges?'

'I eat them, but not this one. I don't want it.'

'Do you think it's bewitched and both of us will become lizards and scuttle away into a hole?'

She heard herself laughing. 'Okay, let's eat it.'

Another rock and roll song could be heard from Mbambo's radio, the volume still high, as if he was celebrating something. Yet otherwise everything seemed so peaceful at that moment, the night sky with its moon and stars, the cool breeze that blew softly against Thenjiwe's cheeks, and the sweet taste of orange in her mouth.

'It's delicious, isn't it?' Samson smiled with pleasure.

Thenjiwe nodded – and then the earth erupted in a massive explosion.

Another explosion quickly followed, and she found herself on the floor inside the hut, with the heavy body of Samson over hers, his arms around her. His mouth was close to hers and it was moving and saying something that Thenjiwe couldn't hear.

Then, in a quick movement, Samson jumped up and pulled the door shut. The room was suddenly very dark. Thenjiwe's ears felt as if they were blocked with water. Panic gripped her. She scrambled up from the floor. Guerrillas! She could hear sharp bursts of gunfire outside the hut like popcorn popping. She also thought she could hear shouts and screams and barking dogs, though it all seemed unreal.

The air was pungent with smoke and through the window they could see the bursting flames of a fire as it spread across the thatched roof of a nearby hut. Children screamed.

'We're not safe here!' Samson shouted. 'There's a hut on fire outside! The flames will spread very quickly.'

He yanked the door open, grabbed her hand and pulled her outside. Thenjiwe had felt herself resist, something telling her that the outside would be even more dangerous, but Samson's hand had been firm, and he pulled her with him. They fled out of the compound. Other blurred figures also crashed through the bushes, children crying pitifully in the moonlit chaos.

At last, after what felt like hours, Thenjiwe and Samsom stumbled into a small gorge. 'It's a good place to hide,' Thenjiwe said breathlessly. 'We can't keep on running like this in the dark.'

The gorge was covered with a soft carpet of grass, the sides covered with small bushes and dry reeds. Samson broke a few branches off the bushes. 'We'll cover ourselves with these,' he said. They lay down, their arms around each other.

Thenjiwe was exhausted, but her senses were highly attuned. In her mind's eye, she could still see the burning hut, the fleeing figures, and hear the gunfire. Slowly, as the scene played and replayed itself in her mind, she realised that the burning hut had been Mbambo's. She began to shiver, and she felt Samson's arms tighten around her, drawing her closer in the silence broken only by crickets and the occasional owl.

Suddenly she froze. Her arms tightened around the young man. 'Shhh,' Samson whispered, 'something's coming.' She held her breath.

It was the sound of many feet, rushing feet, and the reverberations grew louder and louder.

Then people were leaping in and then running across the gorge, dark shadows against the moonlit sky. They were gone as suddenly as they'd appeared. The sound of their passage receded, and was replaced by the rhythmic call of the cicada.

'It was the guerrillas, but they had some people with them,' Samson whispered into Thenjiwe's ear. She felt almost too tired to care. Emotional exhaustion had taken its toll, and now, suddenly, in this unlikely spot with this unlikely man, she felt safe.

Later that night, she was woken by the sound of a helicopter thundering overhead.

'The whites,' Samson said softly.

***

They left at sunrise.

'What are we going to do?' Thenjiwe asked, as Samson picked grass from her hair. They were standing at the lip of the gorge surrounded by tall trees in a heavily wooded part of the forest.

'Let's go back to the compound,' Samson said. 'It'll be safer there.'

'But after what happened last night ... I want to go home!'

'There's fighting everywhere, Thenjiwe. If you go home, you won't escape it. There's a war going on.'

They returned to the compound, to discover that of the thirty men and women who worked at Wildberg Ranch, two were dead, four injured, and eleven missing, of which one was Mbambo.

A search of the villages undertaken by Mr Phillips and a troop of soldiers in the days following the raid, failed to locate the missing ranch workers. It was assumed that they had been taken by the guerrillas to join the liberation army, ZIPRA.

2004

Chapter 14

MaNdlovu sighed, her fingers moving swiftly. Her mind locked into her first months at Wildberg Ranch.

She had fallen in love with Ngwenya and after a romance of two years they had married in 1979 when she turned twenty. She had no regrets. She still loved Ngwenya although her love was more mature. They had both had the instinctive ability to pick themselves up after every setback that life in the city had tossed their way. They did not expect life to be easy, and their current problems could not be avoided.

Their marriage had been stable and without scandal. Maybe Ngwenya had his secret affairs, like most men, but nothing had ever reached her ears.

She had been a faithful wife; the ancestors knew that. It was Ngwenya who had taken her virginity on their wedding night, although her parents had wanted to offer it to Mbambo in exchange for his cows. All these years later, MaNdlovu bristled at the thought.

Ngwenya had given them cows when he had paid *lobola*, but not the fifteen that Mbambo had promised. Ngwenya had so far paid two of the five he had been charged by her parents.

Ngwenya had been considered an educated man at the ranch, though he only had a ZJC certificate, but these days things were different. She wished they'd taken advantage of the many adult education courses offered shortly after Independence, but they hadn't realised the importance of doing so. Now, however, she's determined that her children should have a proper education, no matter what it costs or what sacrifices were needed. And, then, inevitably her thoughts turned to Senzeni and her heart filled with pain.

At that moment, the light suddenly went out. MaNdlovu listened for a moment in the darkness, waiting, and breathing slowly. Her ears are attuned to the night outside. Beneath the silence she hears the faint whistle of a distant train. Something is moving on the rail track that cuts through Emakhandeni and Richmond, maybe people, maybe goods, going to Victoria Falls, or Harare.

When it seems to MaNdlovu that the power is not going to return any time soon, she carefully places her weaving beside her on the bench, and rises to her feet. She goes past the table in the middle of the room to the far wall, her hands outstretched. She has done this many times and knows the way in the darkness.

Reaching the wall, she feels along it and finds the light switch. She flicks it off and on, her face raised to the roof, her eyes open. She parts the curtain beside the light switch and looks out of the window. The street is in darkness, and the tower lights have also gone out.

'Electricity!' It's just another of those erratic power cuts that have become part of the staple diet of the country alongside the regular meals of *isitswhala* and *tshomoliya* . She guesses that it's around midnight, so she double-checks that the front and back doors are locked, and shuffles her feet across the familiar floor to the bedroom.

A few minutes later she's lying on the bed, as Ambition whimpers in his sleep on the floor; her eyes are open, her mind still in turmoil.

Life had been a little bit easier when her husband was working at Perlin Shoes, a job he had got as soon as they moved into the city in 1981, but the factory had closed down in 2001. It was a time when most factories in Bulawayo closed down, hit hard by hyperinflation and the collapse of secondary industries after the farm invasions, and it was not surprising that he couldn't find another job. So Ngwenya had reverted back to being a cobbler. At least the economic downturn meant that more people were having their shoes repaired, as they could no longer afford the ever-rising cost of new ones.

Ngwenya hadn't been doing too badly. At least he'd kept the wolf from the door. Then, out of the blue, Mbambo, who'd disappeared during the raid at the ranch all those years ago, and about whom there'd been all sorts of rumours, had suddenly re-appeared in Lobengula Township, renting a house in their line and becoming their neighbour!

It had been a great surprise for both MaNdlovu and Ngwenya. They, like many people, had written him off as dead, like so many who did not return home at Independence. There had been so many deaths during that long, ugly war.

Even more surprisingly, Mbambo had rebuffed Ngwenya's approach when he had tried to talk to him. And when MaNdlovu met him in the street, which was unavoidable as their houses were so close, he always pretended not to see her. MaNdlovu didn't mind, as she didn't want to have anything to do with him. She understood why Mbambo might not want to talk to them.

But if the man wanted to distance himself from his neighbours, he couldn't escape their humour – even the children were now calling him by his nickname, 3Pac – or their gossip. It was whispered that Mbambo had been a sell-out.

MaNdlovu moves restlessly as her mind recalls past events. What if 3Pac were a sell-out, what would that mean now? Can it have anything to do with her husband's absence? She takes a deep breath and calms herself, and eventually sleep overcomes her.

Chapter 15

MaNdlovu wakes up at cock-crow and her worried mind pounces on her missing husband. The sleeping Ambition is a silent bundle on the floor, lost to another world as the grey shades of dawn slowly dissipate the dark shadows of night.

Clad in her usual morning attire, an old purple night dress over which she's wrapped a brown bathing towel, MaNdlovu does her morning chores with a heavy heart, breaking her usual routine of sweeping the yard first, then washing the dishes and finally cleaning the house.

Instead, she first washes the dishes. Then she takes the two plastic buckets in the kitchen, which always contain water, in case there's a water cut, and empties them over the *tshomoliya* in the vegetable garden. After rinsing the buckets out, she leaves them upended next to the tap.

The sun has not yet risen, but the sky is blushing with its promise. If there's anything that doesn't disappoint in the township, it's the sun. It's always there, steady as a rock; and when it promises to rise, it will do so.

MaNdlovu returns to the house. Ambition is still fast asleep. She pauses, looking down at him. Her eyes are moist with tears. She sniffs and wipes them with the back of her hand. Please come home, Ngwenya, she says in silent prayer.

She takes the grass sweep from the kitchen and goes back outside the house. She fastens the bathing towel tighter around her waist, and starts sweeping the yard.

Usually, on happier mornings, she makes intricate designs on the soft soil, especially in front of the house outside the *delele* hedge, but today she sweeps in quick disorganised strokes.

After sweeping the yard, as the sun finally appears over the rooftops, she stands at the gate looking down Sibambene Street at the other women doing just the same, but she doesn't really see them. She finds herself sweeping the ground around her bare toes, sighs and straightens up. Then her heart misses a beat.

Ngwenya is walking up the street towards her, his head haloed by the soft orange glow of the sun as if he has just stepped out of its unblinking eye.

***

When MaNdlovu saw the approaching figure of her husband, she suppressed the urge to scream and rush towards him. So much had happened that she felt as if he had been gone for weeks or months rather than 24 hours. Relief and anger engage her in waves, so she steadies herself and slips round to the back of the house. When Ngwenya steps into the kitchen, his wife is standing in the middle of the room. She opens her arms and hugs him, pressing her face on his chest. They do not speak.

'Did Ambition come home?' Ngwenya asks after a few minutes. MaNdlovu looks at him, her eyes moist with tears.

'Yes, yes he did. He's still sleeping in the bedroom. But where have you been, and whatever happened to your eye?'

'Wait, wait, I want to see the child first.' Ngwenya quickly steps across the kitchen and into the bedroom. Besides his swollen left eye, MaNdlovu notices that he's limping.

'He's still sleeping.' There's relief in Ngwenya's voice as he collapses onto the sofa stretching his legs out in front of him.

MaNdlovu wipes her eyes with the collar of her nightdress.

'What is it?' There's concern in Ngwenya's voice.

MaNdlovu sniffs again. 'So much has happened. I've been so worried. Where have you been? Let me show you something.' She goes into the bedroom and returns with a yellow plastic bag. She upends it and the two pieces of cloth Ambition had come home wearing the previous afternoon fall at her feet.

'What's all this?'

'Magic charms, I think. When Ambition came home yesterday, he was wearing them.'

'Jesus! This is serious. Where did he get them from?'

'Where else but from the people who are bewitching us? Can't you see that? I went to the *inyanga* yesterday at sunset to consult him and he said I must come back with you.'

'I've never heard of anything like this. Of course, we'll go to the *inyanga* together tomorrow morning once I've rested. We must understand what's going on.'

'And what happened to you?' MaNgwenya's eyes travel over her husband's swollen eye. 'How did you get that limp?'

'The police. Resisting arrest, so they claimed.' He clicks his tongue. MaNdlovu goes to the cupboard, takes out a plastic container, gives it a good shake and pours the thick *mahewu* into a cup, which she hands to Ngwenya. Then she sits down on the bench in front of him. The two pieces of cloth are lying on the floor between them.

'I know our police force can no longer be trusted, but resisting arrest for what?'

Ngwenya takes a long drink, and begins to tell her how he walked the streets looking for Ambition, and how he'd run into a cloud of choking smoke quite unlike anything he'd ever experienced before. 'It ate into my eyes, my nose and throat, as if a million tiny stinging insects had been let loose,' he tells MaNdlovu. 'My nose and eyes ran, and I coughed uncontrollably. It was horrible!'

'Ambition came home like that too!'

'Then we're lucky to be alive, because that smoke is deadly, I tell you, MaNdlovu. It almost paralysed me. Then Mr Nkani yelled at me to take off my shirt, pee into it and press it to my nose. But I couldn't do that, and as I was standing there, choking, a policeman in riot gear appeared through the smoke, and began to chase me.'

'But what had you done?'

'Do you need to have done anything wrong to be chased by our police these days? But old as I am, I showed him clean air. I left him far far behind.

'Then as I fled ... I can't tell you how my heart was burning ... I ran into Mr Nkani again. He was with a group of people singing those crazy songs that insult the President.'

'These are the new songs of the country.'

'It's so difficult to understand Mr Nkani.' Ngwenya takes another sip of the *mahewu* and wipes his mouth with the back of his hand. 'When he was a teacher we thought he couldn't harm even *impukane*. And now he's poking at bees in their hive with his bare finger.'

Ngwenya shakes his head. Then he tells MaNgwenya how, when Mr Nkani's group had been singing the anti-Mugabe songs, another band of men had approached them, singing the same songs and even more loudly.

'And then what happened?' MaNdlovu is entranced.

'The two groups met. *Hayi wena*, I have never seen anything like that, MaNdlovu!'

'What did you see?'

'In a flash, the new group produced revolvers and arrested everybody in Mr Nkani's group, including me, as I was nearby.'

'They were undercover policemen!'

'Exactly. But Mr Nkani somehow managed to elude them.' There's surprise in Ngwenya's voice as if the teacher's disappearance has just occurred in their kitchen.

'He has juju!'

'You know I'm beginning to suspect so too, MaNdlovu. That man is doing too many dangerous things and you can't escape all the time. There has to be something else. He must be seeing a very powerful *inyanga*.'

'Or maybe he was just born lucky.'

'Maybe,' Ngwenya shrugs his shoulders. 'Who knows ...'

Then he explains to his wife how he tried to reason with the police. 'I told them that I was a harmless father looking for his little boy, but my plea fell on deaf ears, and I received a beating with handcuffs from one of them. Then they took us to the police station and locked us in a cell.

'But luckily for me, Ntando's father was on duty this morning. And the moment he saw me, he had me released. He's such a good man and good neighbour. He told me that the poisonous smoke is called tear gas. The police use it to break up demonstrations!'

'*Hawu!* I've heard people talking about it. There were mortars and AK-47s during the war, but no tear gas, or none that we knew of.'

With her husband's story finished, MaNdlovu tells him about the petrol bombing of Mr Nkani's house, and how Mrs Nkani had said that she'd seen Senzeni throwing the bomb.

'Do you think it's true?'

'I'm still shocked. I just don't know.'

'If Mrs Nkani says she saw Senzeni do it, then I believe her,' Ngwenya says. 'Everybody in the township knows that she's running around with the Green Bombers.'

'But what are we going to do? We must do something, for God's sake.'

'There's nothing that I can think of right now. We've tried everything and failed. Sometimes things have a way of resolving themselves. The spirits are there and they are watching.'

Chapter 16

It's another very hot day and life seems to stand still. Ngwenya, in the lead, walks along Sibambene Street. He's carrying a faded orange travelling bag. Ambition follows close behind him and MaNdlovu brings up the rear.

No one speaks. Ambition's eyes are on the faded white lettering on the broad back of his father's blue overalls: ANGLO AMERICAN PLATI-NUM.

'We're going to do something important in the bush that will help all of us.' Ngwenya had gravely informed Ambition before they left home. 'It will especially help you, my son, after whatever occurred to you two days ago.'

When his mother had woken him up, she'd told him that she and his father were going to consult the *inyanga*, and that he was not to go anywhere until they returned. Ambition had felt his heart lighten. The *inyanga* with his razor blade was the last person he wanted to see.

When his parents had departed, he got dressed and washed his face at the tap. Then he'd found some warm porridge in the pot on the stove, served himself a plateful, added peanut butter and sugar to it, and had his breakfast.

Two hours later, his parents had come back and found him trying to construct a car from wire in the shade of the mulberry tree.

'I want you to listen carefully,' his father said. 'The *inyanga* has given us something important to do. We're going to walk across the township into the bush. You must not look behind you or to the side, or talk to anyone, even if we know them and even if they greet us.'

Ambition had nodded, intrigued.

'If you look behind you or talk to anyone, the magic won't work. Do you understand me?'

Ambition had nodded his head again, and then had asked in a small voice. 'Are we going to meet the *inyanga* in the forest Baba?'

His father had looked into his eyes. 'You're afraid of him?'

'Yes, Baba, I do not like his razor blade.'

'That's good. It shows that you have fear, which I sometimes doubt judging by the things you get up to. But, no, my son, this time we will work without the *inyanga*, but at his instruction.'

'No razor blade?'

'No razor blade, I promise you, unless you disobey me, then we will be forced to call the *inyanga* to come with it.'

As they walk through the township, Ginger suddenly appears at his father's feet, and his father kicks him away. The dog yelps and disappears behind Ambition, who almost turns his head, but remembering his father's warning, keeps his eyes fixed firmly ahead.

'How are you, Baba Ngwenya?' A female voice calls from behind them. 'MaNdlovu, how is the child?'

Ambition instantly recognises the voice of MaChivanda. Nobody replies and the Ngwenya family walks on as if they've not heard anything. Ambition hunches his shoulders. He feels very rude. Thankfully, MaChivanda does not call out again.

They walk on. The yards that line the street seem empty, except for a child here and there, and they are of no concern to the Ngwenya family. Ambition is relieved that Ntando is nowhere to be seen. His friend would never have understood an apparent rebuff.

As they reach the end of the street, Ntando's father, Tshabalala, appears in front of them. He's dressed in riot police uniform, and carries a long truncheon in one hand, and a plastic carrier bag containing several bottles of beer in the other. He's wearing a dark blue helmet with the plastic visor pulled up. As he draws nearer, he tucks his truncheon into his armpit, and takes off his helmet. His face is covered in sweat. 'Good morning, good neighbours,' he greets them in a tired voice, and tries to wipe his face against his right shoulder, then his jaw drops as the Ngwenya family walk past him without replying.

So this is the beginning, Sergeant Tshabalala thinks as he watches the Ngwenya family. He'd expected that his neighbours would begin to shun him ever since the election business and the riots had begun, and the police had been ordered into the streets and told to beat people up.

But to think that only yesterday he'd helped Ngwenya obtain his release without any charges being preferred against him ... surely he did not now deserve to be ignored? He wonders what it will be like at the bottle store. He'd been looking forward to going there. He was off duty for two whole days and he'd planned to drink them away, as he'd just received some money from his wife in the UK.

To hell with with his police job! He would go home, drink the beers he had with him and then go to the bottle store so as to arrive there already in full swing.

***

The Ngwenya family walk through Lobengula Township, across the Masiyephambili Road, and along Ntatshana Hill towards Njube Township. When they reach the Emagetsini Power Station, they turn right and cross Luveve Road into Emakhandeni Township. There they skirt the Power Station, entering the open land between Emakhandeni and Entumbane. The walk had taken them no more than twenty minutes.

They walk past a cluster of giant boulders and a clump of thorn bushes. Finally, Ngwenya comes to a stop where the path splits in two. They're alone and the bush seems eerily silent. 'This will do,' his father says in a low voice. 'Let's be quick before anyone comes this way.'

MaNdlovu nods her head. Ambition thinks that her solemn expression makes her look as if she's standing in front of the headmaster of his school. His father opens his bag and takes out the two pieces of cloth with which the priest Siziba had adorned Ambition's body and in which he'd fled home.

Ngwenya places both pieces of cloth at the crux of the fork on the path. Then he takes a plastic Mazoe bottle containing a mix of water and herbs. He shakes the bottle, and removes the top. Ambition hears a slight fizzing sound.

'Come here,' he tells Ambition.

'Don't be afraid, Ambition,' his mother says. 'Nobody's going to harm you.'

Ambition nods his head.

'I want you to take this liquid into your mouth,' his father tells him. 'Don't swallow it, but spit it on those pieces of cloth.'

'But father those things belong to ...'

'Please don't talk, Ambition,' his mother admonishes him. 'Just listen to what your father is telling you.'

Ambition opens his mouth, and his father pours a little liquid into it. Ambition tries not to swallow. The mixture tastes of a bitter root. He can feel it begin to dribble from the sides of his mouth.

'Now spit,' his father instructs him.

Ambition spits at the pieces of cloth, and then watches in fascination. He expects something to happen to them, but nothing does. He hears his father give a soft grunt of satisfaction, as he passes the plastic container to his mother.

MaNdlovu takes a mouthful, swills it, and then shoots the liquid out, as if by this action she is condemning the two small pieces of cloth, and all the bad luck they represent, to death.

She passes the bottle back to Ngwenya, who takes a mouthful, spits at the cloth, and then pours the remaining liquid over them, intoning, 'We don't know what we've done to deserve this, spirits of our forefathers. All we're asking is that whoever is doing this to us, please leave us in peace so that our children can grow up into a happy future.'

Ngwenya then up-ends the bottle and places it next to the sodden cloth.

'It's done. We can go home now.' He sounds pleased and relieved.

A whirlwind suddenly springs up. There's a loud noise and Ginger races toward them from behind a bush, chasing a lizard, which streaks up a tree out of reach, and Ginger begins to bark.

'*Haibo*, this dog!' Ngwenya exclaims. 'Thankfully, it can't talk otherwise it would spread rumours all over the township.'

With that, Ngwenya turns and they follow him back through the bush. Ambition in the rear, Ginger at his side. This time the family looks freely about them, relief in their hearts.

Chapter 17

The staple diet of the township is *isitshwala* with a relish of *tshomoliya*. If there's money, meat's added, and if the relish is properly cooked, it provides a tasty meal. *Isitshwala* is unchanging, but the relish will vary depending on what's available in the vegetable garden. For those in the know, the customary *delele* hedge is also edible. Its tender leaves can be cooked to make a relish, especially if there's no money for other options, and the garden is barren.

There's *tshomoliya* in MaNdlovu's garden, and a ball of cabbage and dried caterpillars in the house, but this morning she's decided that they must have *idelele* for lunch, just for a change. Her husband has promised to bring home some meat for supper.

As she plucks the leaves, she sees Ambition leave the house carrying a plastic ball. He's dressed in black jogger shorts with a white stripe at the side, and a white T-shirt with a black 9 at the front, his Highlanders soccer kit. Despite the relief that she feels after the exorcism ceremony, MaNdlovu does not want her son much out her sight, and she knows that a game of street soccer can last until sunset.

'I'm not going far, Mama, I'm just visiting Ntando,' he responds to her raised eyebrows.

'But, Ambi, what you're wearing tells me a different story.'

'Sure, Mama,' Ambition smiles. 'Trust me.' He throws the ball into the air and kicks it at the hedge, aiming for the hole.

'I don't know who can explain to you and Ntando not to play so far away from home. We worry when we can't find you.'

'Don't worry, Mama.' Ambition walks to the hedge, picks up the ball, crouches down and vanishes through the hole. 'I'll be around,' he says as he disappears.

Emerging on the other side, Ambition sees Ntando peeping through the window of his home. Suddenly his friend raises a fist in the air in triumph. Ambition steals up behind him.

'Now, Freeman! Now!' Ntando hisses quietly. He's on tiptoe.

'Now for what?' Ambition whispers, and elbows Ntando aside.

His body stiffens. Through the small hole in the curtain on the window, he can see Freeman, Ntando's brother. His arms are locked around a girl. Ambition's mouth opens in dismay. It's Nobuhle.

An only child, Nobuhle is a student nurse, living with her grandmother, MaDlodlo. Both her parents are migrant workers in South Africa – and they send enough money and groceries for Nobuhle and her grandmother to live comfortable lives.

To Ambition, Nobuhle is the most beautiful girl in the world who, in her white nursing uniform, seems like an angel. His mother affectionately calls Nobuhle her daughter-in-law, which makes Ambition thrill with shyness, and Nobuhle often teases him saying that he'll never be able to propose to a girl when he grows up.

'What are they doing now?' Ntando hisses, as the boys jostle each other to peep through the curtain. But Ambition has had enough. He runs towards his yard and dives through the hole in the hedge, with Ntando hot on his heels, and then out into the street.

'I think he saw me,' Ambition says. 'He was looking straight at me.'

'No ways!' Ntando grabs the ball from Ambition. 'He might have seen your eye but not you. You can't tell who a person is by their eyes – unless you're Power.' He giggles at his joke.

'You shouldn't peep at your brother, Ntando. You'll grow boils in your eyes, don't you know that?'

'But you also peeped.' Ntando throws the ball, his foot thwacks into it and it arcs and bounces to the ground.

'I'm older than you and I do not grow boils that easily,' Ambition says. 'Don't you know that?' And the two boys sprint after the ball.

***

The *delele* Ambition's mother had prepared for lunch with *isitshwala*, which Ambition had shared with Ntando, had not been too bad, and after lunch MaNdlovu had sent them to Ilanga Youth Centre.

The Centre had once been a place where talent of all kinds was identified and nurtured. But in the years after Independence, the City Council, for reasons best known, chose to run vocational training projects in some youth centres and close others down. They locked the doors on Ilanga Youth Centre, but the Green Bombers knocked down the gate and doors, and transformed it into their terror camp or 'base'. And it's there that Senzeni is sitting on a stone under a tall gum tree inside the fence; Ambition and Ntando are on the other side. They've come with a message from MaNdlovu.

'What did she say?' Senzeni asks impatiently.

A short distance away inside the fence a group of boys and girls are playing soccer, all the players going after the ball like a swarm of bees.

Another group sits under another tree at the side of the soccer pitch, watching the game and drinking something from a bottle which they are passing around. They are all dressed in green.

'She said that you must wake up,' Ambition replies.

'Is that what she sent you all this way to tell me?' Senzeni's eyes move rapidly this way and that. Her look has a hard edge, one not often found in a sixteen-year-old girl.

Ambition nods his head.

'That woman does not know about Pan Africa,' Senzeni says. 'Do you two know what Pan Africa is?'

'We have two at home,' Ntando answers.

'Two what?'

'Two pans, one for frying sausages and one for eggs,' replies Ntando. 'My mother sent us them from London.'

'Talking with you is useless,' Senzeni says impatiently. 'But Pan Africa is going to rule this country, not those white-skinned thieves you township people worship so much who want to steal our land.'

'Have you been given land, Senzeni?' Ambition loves his sister, but he's afraid of her in this new guise, and he senses that beneath the bravado, she might also be a little afraid.

'I don't need to be given land, all the land in this country is mine, and nobody is going to steal it as long as I live.'

'How about a tractor, Senzeni?' Ntando asks eagerly. 'I want to ride on one when it's ploughing. Brm Brm.'

Senzeni looks straight at Ntando. 'Your mother ran away to the UK. She sends you money, but can't you see she has put your father in a tight spot? What does he say when other policemen ask him where his wife is? If I was him, I would phone her and tell her to come home immediately.

Anyone who's left the country is a sell-out!'

'Mother told me on the phone that she's not coming back,' Ntando says. 'Do you want us to starve like other people? Instead, my mother is going to send our family money to get passports and we are going to fly in an aeroplane and join her in London.'

'Then she's a very big sell-out, and you should be ashamed!'

'She's not.'

'She is.'

'I'm going to tell father you said that.'

'You go and tell him right now, and also tell him he can find me here waiting for him.'

'He's a policeman and you're nothing but a Green Bomber.'

'Just shut up, stupid.'

'Mother said I must give you this.' Ambition breaks into the conversation, holding up a yellow plastic bag that they've brought with them.

'What's inside? Food? Good...' Senzeni's voice drops to a whisper. 'These people are really starving us here!'

Ntando laughs. 'I told you Senzeni, we've never starved, mother sends us pounds and we change them in MaChivanda's home and get a lot of Zimbabwean dollars.'

Senzeni scowls at Ntando, and Ambition interjects, 'Mother says she can't send you food now because there's not enough at home. But you can come and eat with us any time you like, if you're hungry.'

'When you've finished beating up people,' Ntando adds mischievously. He chuckles and boxes the air in front of him with the plastic ball.

Senzeni stands up and leans against the fence. 'Please throw the bag over.'

Ambition throws the bag over the fence. Senzeni catches and opens it and takes out a neatly folded cream T-shirt.

'What's this?' she holds the T-shirt up.

'It's yours,' Ambition says. 'The one you bought at the flea market. Have you forgotten already?'

'But why did mother send it to me?'

'Maybe she wants you to change.' Ambition looks critically at the green T-shirt his sister's wearing.

'Change?' Anger fills Senzeni's face. She stuffs the T-shirt back in the plastic bag, and lobs the parcel over the fence. 'Take it back,' she yells furiously. 'Tell her that will never happen. I'll never change. Why should I? Is mother saying I'm dirty and I smell? I know! This is not about clothing, it's a message, isn't it?'

'No, it's not, Senzeni.' Ambition's gaze is fixed on his sister. He thinks she's trying not to cry. 'It's only that when you ran away from home, you didn't take any clothes with you. Look how dirty your T-shirt is.'

'I'm doing *real* work here and there's no time to behave like a silly girl. I'm doing political work, not going to church and praying to God to do it for me! The time for me to dress up will come soon, I promise you.' Her voice drops. 'I'm on to something powerful now, my dear brother, just wait and see. My future is all but confirmed. And I did it on my own after my very own parents chased me from home.' Her mouth tightens. 'Imagine that, my own parents!'

Ambition is silent. The air is filled with sounds of the football game behind Senzeni.

'Why are you staring at me, Ambition? Don't you believe me?'

Her brother ignores her question. 'What should I tell mother?'

'Exactly what I told you the last time you were here. I have a new family now, and it's too late. I will never come home!' Her voice softens as if she's heard what she's said for the first time. 'But you and Ntando are my boys and I will take care of you when things normalise and we win the votes in the coming elections.' She takes a bundle of bearer cheques from her jeans pocket, peels off a bill and hands it to Ambition through the fence. 'There, you can go and play slug at the shops.'

Ambition looks at the note for five million dollars, just enough for a game of slug.

'Come and visit me any time, Comrades,' Senzeni tells them. 'And lastly, Ambition, I know father and mother like to consult the *inyanga* when things are not going right in the house. Please tell them that they can forget about the *inyanga* – even *muti* won't work to make me come home. You can go now.' She gives them a salute, then turns and heads towards the open field behind her.

The soccer game is over and the group is assembling into a marching line while a man with a hatchet-like face and a black beret barks instructions.

Chapter 18

'She gave us money.' Ambition shows the note to his mother, who stands beside the *tshomoliya* patch, a hoe beside her. 'She said we can play slug with it.'

I'm going to beat Ambition ten to one, he doesn't know how to play,' Ntando grinned.

'Can somebody please tell me where Senzeni got that money from when even the banks have no cash?' MaNdlovu holds out her hand. 'Give it to me, Ambition.'

She grasps the note, which has a red stain in one corner. '*Mayiwe*, there's blood on it! I might have known! This is stolen money. Stolen from one of the people they've beaten up! This note carries bad luck! We won't have anything to do with it.' She tears the bearer's cheque into tiny bits, walks over to the refuse bin and throws them in. Ambition's eyes shine with tears.

'Please don't cry, Ambi, you and Ntando can go and play soccer. It's better than slug. It gives you more exercise. Now, wipe those tears away. I keep telling you that you're no longer a little boy.' MaNdlovu picks up her hoe. 'Ambition? The T-shirt – did your sister take it?'

'She refused.' Ambition holds out the plastic bag.

'That stupid girl!' MaNdlovu takes the bag. 'How can she wear that same green T-shirt for weeks on end! She's not a *tshomoliya* leaf? I'm trying to help her and she doesn't even see it!'

'She said even if you use *muti*, it won't work on her.'

'*Muti?*' MaNdlovu raises the plastic bag in the air and shakes it. 'This is not *muti*, but her T-shirt! She bought it from the flea market last year with her own money.'

It had been MaChivanda who'd given Senzeni the money after she'd

72

helped their neighbour with her forex customers, counting bearer's cheques. Senzeni had gone to Entumbane Flea Market with Ambition and Ntando and bought the T-shirt as a treat to herself.

'How can I bewitch my own child? How can she think this way?' MaNdlovu's voice rose. Ntando quickly changed the subject.

'She told us they're all hungry at the camp. They don't get enough food.'

'Did she really say that?'

'Yes she did. If there's any food in the house, Ntando and I can take it to her.'

'She won't refuse food like she did the T-shirt,' Ntando adds. 'Hunger isn't like wearing something.'

'Okay, I'll tell you what, there's a little *delele* and *isitshwala* left over from lunch; let me put it into a scoff tin and you can take it to her.

'And Ambition, please don't tell your father that I sent you to Senzeni with food, like you did last week, okay? You know how angry he can get.'

On that occasion, Ambition had delivered Senzeni's old bath towel and a piece of soap, because MaNdlovu had worried that her daughter would catch a bad skin disease from sharing a towel. But her father had been adamant.

'She fled from home,' he had told his wife, finality in his voice. 'So why should you care for her, if she doesn't care for us? Never, ever send her anything behind my back, do you hear me?'

No one had replied and he'd taken the silence for consent.

***

When the two boys reach Ilanga Youth Centre again, they find the militia training in the middle of the football pitch and marching up and down like soldiers. The man with the black beret is marching at their side, shouting in a loud voice: 'Lef' ra', lef' ra', lef' ra', lef' ra',' as the feet of the militia rise and fall, almost in unison.

Ntando holds the scoff tin and Ambition the T-shirt, as they stand at the fence. And this time they're not the only ones, for lots of children are standing gawking at the Green Bombers. It's only when the militia storms out of the Youth Centre on the rampage that everyone disappears. On such days, the militia always give themselves a head start with a large dose of alcohol and plenty of *mbanje*. Once drunk, they begin singing revolutionary songs, and that's the moment to vanish.

Ambition can see Senzeni clearly as the line of marchers comes towards them. She's at the head, carrying the flag high over her head.

Senzeni had once been a drum majorette at primary school; she had been chosen several times to go to the Trade Fair and Independence celebrations to lead the school team. It seems to Ambition that his sister marches better than all the other militias in the two lines coming behind her. Her body is so straight, it seems to slant backwards, and she is holding the flag like soldiers hold their rifles. Her face is serious, but her step is jaunty. 'Lef' righ', lef' righ', lef' righ', lef' righ.'

'Should I call her, Ambi?'

'Not yet Ntando, can't you see they're marching?'

'But we can't wait here all day.'

'Let's just wait a bit longer. I think she's seen us; as soon as she gets a chance, she'll come over and find out why we're here.'

***

When Senzeni had run away from home, no one knew where she had gone, and a funereal cloud hung over Ambition's home.

He remembered how hard they'd searched for her. They'd walked the streets, calling her, hoping that she was hiding somewhere within earshot, but their calls had only met with curious glances from passersby.

Then his mother had suggested that they visit Mavis. She was the same age as Senzeni, and the two girls had become friends at primary school where they had both been in the netball team. However, Mavis was always in the 'A' classes, as she excelled in her studies, and Senzeni was always in the 'C's – until she had dropped to 'D' because of bad grades.

Mavis and her mother, MaNcube, had talked to Senzeni's family over their gate. 'I haven't seen her for some months now,' Mavis told them.

'I told her to stop seeing Senzeni when she dropped out of school,' MaNcube added smugly. 'I like Senzeni, and my daughter likes her too, but Mavis is working hard and I don't want her to have friends with another agenda. I have to be careful, because my husband works outside the country, and I can't take risks.'

'We understand, MaNcube,' his mother had responded kindly. 'But since Senzeni has not come home, we just thought we should ask Mavis as they were such good friends once.'

'And there's no one else she might have gone to?' asked Ngwenya.

Mavis shook her head. MaNcube, perhaps regretting her complacency, suggested that perhaps they go to the police. Ngwenya shook his head. Senzeni had only been gone four hours. He reflected that he'd intended to give her a beating she would never forget, but her absence was a consequence that he had not anticipated.

They had walked home in silence, each wrapped in thoughts that they could not express.

Senzeni had still not returned the following day. Ngwenya had gone to the police to make a report. Ambition heard the sadness and the worry in his mother's voice, for that was how he felt too; something hot and swollen seemed to be sitting in his throat.

His father had come home complaining that the police were useless. 'They told me I just had to wait.'

'What did you expect them to do?'

'What did I expect them to do, MaNdlovu? Well, more than just tell me to come back in two days if we've still not found the child. Aren't they trained to search for missing people?'

***

School had been horrible too. Mrs Gumbo was at her meanest, and had given them a tough maths exercise, rapping pupils on their knuckles with the chalkboard duster for giving the wrong answers. Ambition had only got two questions wrong, so he'd only received two raps, but they'd been painful. Usually he could take up to five raps without tears, but he'd found himself trying to brush them away with the back of his hand before anyone noticed.

When he returned home, he realised that his father had not gone to work but had spent the day alternately sitting in the shade of the mulberry tree, and searching for Senzeni. It was the same the next day. In fact, some of his customers had come looking for him because they wanted their shoes back. To make things worse, at least that's how it seemed to Ambition, their neighbours began to come and offer sympathy, as if Senzeni had died. And so the days had passed with a steady stream of visitors either searching for their shoes, or offering condolences.

On Sunday MaChivanda had offered to conduct a prayer service at their home with her church members, but his father had politely declined. Instead, he had gone to see the *inyanga*. On his return he and his wife had closed themselves in the house after asking Ambition to go outside. He did not like sitting in the yard, and could not imagine what they were up to that he should not know about, but the smell had revealed that they'd been burning herbs.

But maybe it was the herbs that helped, for that night as they sat in silence in the kitchen, they heard the sound of heavy feet and then a knock at the door. It was Mrs Gumbo.

'I'm not staying long,' she announced, as she breezed into the room and sat down beside his mother on the bench. 'I have heard about your matter, Baba Ngwenya. That you can't find your daughter.'

His father nodded. He was not sympathetic to anyone he thought of as an intruder or a busybody.

'But what happened? Why did she run away from home? Did you hit her?'

Ambition thought this was a bit rich, given how hard Mrs Gumbo beat the children in her class.

'There was a slight family misunderstanding, and I guess she got angry,' his father had responded evasively.

'Whatever it was, please see that does not happen again. Children need understanding. That way you won't have problems with them. Look at Ambition.' Mrs Gumbo hectored like an adult speaking to children. 'Every child in my class is obedient. Ask yourself why? Because I talk to them, and understand their needs. On the other hand, look at Mr Nkani's products, all his students are running wild.'

'We understand, Mrs Gumbo,' his mother said patiently, and before Mrs Gumbo infuriated her husband any further. 'We will be careful when Senzeni comes home, but we have to find her first.'

'You don't need to look far ...' Mrs Gumbo had saved her *coup de grace* till last 'She has joined the National Youth Service programme.'

'Oh no!' MaNdlovu gasped.

'She's there at Ilanga Youth Centre. I was told by a friend who's a trainer there, so I thought I should come and tell you to ease your stressed minds. Good people, goodnight.' She turned abruptly towards Ambition. 'See you at school, boy! Make sure you get your homework done.' Then she was gone, her duty done.

Ambition had felt a flood of relief the moment he knew Senzeni was alive, and he turned to look at his parents with a smile, as he heard Mrs Gumbo shut the door behind her. But instead of looking relieved, his father and mother seemed to look even grimmer than before.

'God save us,' his mother said.

'What is it, Mama?' Ambition asked with a new sense of dread.

'Your sister has joined the Green Bombers, that's the National Youth Service, and it can only mean trouble for us,' his father replied.

Chapter 19

The matter of his wife's missing underwear had caused Ngwenya acute embarrassment, so quickly had it become a public joke at the Easy Way Bottle Store. Ngwenya felt so bad that had he been a lodger he would have moved away from the township. But since he owned his house and had a family, all he could do was turn up his collar and weather the ridicule and the laughter.

He'd considered moving from under the shade of the mango tree just in front of the bottle store, but he'd developed a loyal clientele there, and knew that he'd lose at least some of them if he moved, and he didn't have the energy to start again.

He cursed the day Mbambo had also come to mend shoes at the shopping centre, for it had been Mbambo who'd told the story of the petticoat and turned something small into a comedy that had made the whole township laugh, or so it seemed to Ngwenya.

Ngwenya arcs his back as he feels a twinge of pain in his spine. His eyes travel across the shopping centre, the supermarket, the bottle store, and the line of vegetable vendors, then slowly he bends back over the shoe he's mending.

His back has been giving him problems for years and nothing seems to help, not painkillers or *inyanga's muti*. Inevitably, MaChivanda had offered to pray over him, but his pride would not let him. Pride and disbelief. MaChivanda was essentially a money-changer, and everyone in her church seemed to put money beyond all else. But hadn't Jesus driven the money-changers out of the Temple in Jerusalem?

He studies the boot he's mending, which belongs to the milkman, Peace. What a name to have in this day and age! He'd refused to work on the boot when Peace had given it to him, because it was so tattered, but Peace had pleaded with him, and Ngwenya had finally relented after extracting a promise that if the boot fell apart under his needle, he could not be held accountable.

Had Ngwenya not needed every cent, he would certainly not have tried to mend the boot, because Peace had intimated that Mbambo had been telling stories about Ngwenya, as if it was not enough to set up in competition. But before Ngwenya had been able to find out more, Mbambo had emerged from the bottle store, beer in hand, MaVundla trailing him angrily.

'I want my money!' she had shouted furiously.

'You're crazy!' Mbambo had opened the bottle with his teeth, sat down behind his pile of shoes, picked one up and started working on it.

'I wish she'd beat him up,' Peace had said. 'I'd help her do it. Once when you weren't here, I gave him my child's school shoes to repair, and he lost – or sold – them! One day, I'll get my own back.'

Ngwenya shakes his head. It seems to him today that the world is full of deceipt, backstabbing, meanness and jealousy, and he wonders if it's the situation, or if it has always been like this.

***

Mbambo operates from the best position of the shopping centre pavement, just beside the door of the supermarket. Ngwenya had tried for many years to get permission from Mr Sozinto, the owner of the shopping centre, to operate from the pavement, as it was protected from the elements. But Mr Sozinto had flatly refused, claiming that vendors made the pavement cluttered and dirty.

Then, one day, Mbambo had simply installed himself, and set up his shoe-mending accoutrements in the space between the bottle store and supermarket doors, and no one had turned him away. That had been a year and a half ago. At the time, Ngwenya had watched in surprise. How could it be that after twenty-four years Thunder Mbambo, the foreman of Wildberg Ranch, who'd disappeared after the guerrilla attack, should set himself up as a shoemaker outside a supermarket? How could it be that Mr Sozinto didn't evict him? And why, when he had the whole township to choose from, should he start mending shoes just metres away from Ngwenya's stall?

1977

Chapter 20

After the attack on the ranch and the disappearance of Mbambo and others, Ngwenya had been elevated to the position of foreman by Mr Phillips, and eleven workers had also been hired from the surrounding villages.

Ngwenya was offered what had been Mbambo's hut, after it had been repaired. The hut was spacious and came with an iron bed, a small table, two chairs and a paraffin stove. As foreman, he discovered that he now had more time on his hands; his duties were more supervisory, and the workers did not need much supervision.

He also found himself visiting the ranch house more often than before, to report to the Phillipses. This, of course, meant seeing more of Senzeni, who he considered a warm-hearted young woman with a quick and inquisitive mind.

'When do you think it is going to end?' she'd asked him one day as he waited to see Mrs Phillips. 'The war I mean?'

'Who knows?' Ngwenya shrugged his shoulders. 'I guess it'll be over when the brothers eventually win.'

'It's not only men who are fighting!'

'Oh, sorry, when the brothers and sisters win.'

'But are they going to win?' They were talking in low voices as Tom pushed a toy tank across the floor of the veranda, making shooting sounds with his mouth. 'They've been fighting for years now, and white people are still ruling the country.' She nodded her head in Tom's direction.

Ngwenya glanced at the small boy. 'Almost the whole of Africa is now free, and the countries fought for their freedom.' His voice was so low she could barely hear him. 'It's the only way forward. The whites are greatly outnumbered. They will lose in time. It's inevitable.'

'Have you ever thought of joining up?'

'On whose side?' Ngwenya avoided eye contact, looking at the tip of his boots.

'Whose side would you fight on?'

He looked up at her, and she looked down at her hands, which were still clasped on her lap.

'It's pretty obvious isn't it?' he replied.

'No, you tell me. There are plenty of blacks in the Rhodesian army.'

Her words seemed to say that while some blacks were in the national army fighting the guerrillas, here they were, working in a white ranch.

'Well, you make a guess!' His voice was hard. She'd pushed too far and he'd taken offence. He knew that she knew the answer and he didn't have to say it; if she didn't know it, then she might be suspecting him of something unpleasant. But before he could reply, the door onto the veranda opened, and Mrs Phillips appeared.

'What are you two whispering about?' She was carrying a glass of beer, a rifle slung over her shoulder. She was never unarmed when her husband was away. Losing her son and daughter-in-law had simultaneously hardened and frightened her.

'Nothing madam,' Ngwenya replied, jumping to his feet, and pressing his sun hat to his chest, his face expressionless. 'We talk of sun and how hot he is.'

'Yes, it's pretty obvious *he* is hot?' Mrs Phillips sounded irritated. She looked at Tom, and then knelt beside him and ruffled his hair.

'Okay, Tommy?'

'My tank needs new bullets.'

'Don't worry sonny, we'll fill her up when we drive to the city tomorrow.'

'And new wheels, too. I want to drive the tank around the ranch.'

'Big wheels to chase the small-minded terrorists, hmm?' Mrs Phillips switched to Ndebele as she turned to Senzeni, 'Everything okay?'

'Yes madam, no problem at all.' Senzeni flashed her an empty smile.

Mrs Phillips looked at Ngwenya. 'Come in. Let's hear your story. Are there any signs of the two missing cows?'

'No, nothing...' Ngwenya followed her into the house. Two cows had gone missing three days previously from Paddock Four. The fence surrounding the paddock had been cut and the animals spirited out of the ranch. Mrs Phillips had ordered Ngwenya to take Gumede, an expert tracker, to track the cattle thieves, whom she suspected might be neighbouring villagers.

Ngwenya and Gumede had followed the spoor, which led them deep into the countryside to the south-west. They had both taken off their ranch overalls in case they met the guerrillas, whose reaction towards people who worked for whites was often unpredictable.

At sunset, they'd crossed a dry streambed, still following the spoor, when a man appeared from behind a clump of bushes, his right hand raised for them to stop. He was dressed in rice camouflage, an AK-47 hung by a strap across his chest, and he wore a pair of large sunglasses and a black beret.

'You can call me Never-Say-Never,' the man had introduced himself. 'I have a question for you gentlemen.' Ngwenya and Gumede looked at each other in electrified silence 'Where are you going to in such a rush?'

Ngwenya had looked at Gumede – Gumede had also been looking at him.

'I asked where you're going, brothers?' Never-Say-Never's right hand slid down to the butt of his AK-47.

'We've heard there's a homestead selling *skokiaan* somewhere near here, my son,' Gumede responded quickly. 'We want to buy some as we understand it's the best there is.'

'And how are you going to carry it back to Wildberg Ranch?' Never-Say-Never said flatly and much to Ngwenya's horror. 'I don't see that you have any containers with you, Gumede.'

'We're going to drink it there and then,' Ngwenya heard himself saying. 'Alcohol is not allowed at the ranch.' If this guerrilla knows Gumede by name, he thought, he will certainly know who I am.

'You know how stupid white people can be about things that don't concern them,' Gumede added. 'But come rain or shine, we'll win this war, thanks to brave sons like you.'

'Do you want me to shoot both of you, *mdala*?'

Gumede stared at Never-Say-Never. 'Why would you shoot an old man like me, if I may be allowed to ask, *mtanami*?'

'Don't lie when you're spoken to,' Never-Say-Never said sharply. He turned to Ngwenya and addressed him by name. 'As the foreman of *abantu* at the ranch, I want you to listen closely, as I won't repeat it.'

Ngwenya nodded his head.

'As the new foreman of Wildberg,' Never-Say-Never repeated, 'the ZIPRA forces expect you *not* to follow us when we take cattle from the ranch. We do not steal! We take. Do you understand that?'

Ngwenya had nodded his head.

'Speak up!'

'Yes I do, Sir.'

'Good. Now you sound like a man. I hate people with no confidence. They make me feel bad, especially given what we're trying to achieve. We're fighting a very dangerous war. We are fighting it for you – and what are you doing?'

There was silence. A flight of noisy birds swooped onto an *mvimila* tree and the air was filled with their chatter. It was strange that sometimes the earth seemed at its most beautiful at its most dangerous moments, and mankind a blessed species.

Ngwenya's lips were dry, but he feared to lick them in case he sent the wrong signal by appearing indifferent to the guerrilla.

Never-Say-Never broke the silence. 'It's a difficult question, isn't it?' There was a thin smile on his lips, as if he were aware of the discomfort he'd caused the two men. 'Let's be clear. We're fighting a war while you live in comfort with the enemy. Nonetheless, the cattle from Wildberg will feed that war. Your duty is to divert the whites whenever we take their cattle. Do you understand me?'

'Yes, yes, we understand,' Ngwenya nodded his head, feeling that the dangerous moment had passed. 'Actually, we had no intention of catching up with the people who took the cattle; we knew it was ZIPRA, and we all support you.'

Never-Say-Never was silent for a moment. They all knew that there was no way the two men could have known from the spoor alone that the cattle had been taken by the guerrilla army. Ngwenya shifted uncomfortably under Never-say-Never's gaze. He was unaccustomed to lying.

The birds on the tree continued to squawk at each other. Then the guerrilla spoke. 'We asked your previous foreman Mbambo the same question. We requested that he co-operate with us. Instead, he sold us out to the regime. He gave them our camp position in the mountains and they attacked us.'

Ngwenya and Gumede exchanged an astonished look.

'Three of our comrades were killed,' Never-Say-Never went on. 'They were brave sons of some of our own relatives, comrades who were determined to end the rule of this sinful white regime. After the attack we looked for Mbambo at his homestead. We wanted him to suffer a painful death as a lesson to all like-minded villagers, but he'd fled back to your ranch. That attack on the ranch that nearly took your lives was aimed at him, but the rat managed to escape. Once we catch him, however, he'll learn what traitors deserve. So, be warned. Unnecessary bloodshed is not our design, but if needs be, ZIPRA is prepared. We want to see this country liberated. This war has been going on for too long and the toll on us is a heavy one. We're also people just like you.'

Silence fell between the three men. Ngwenya remembered the two helicopters he'd seen fly over the ranch the day before Mbambo returned a month early from his vacation; he remembered the distant sound of gunfire.

'We sympathise with the comrades who fell during the raid,' Gumede broke the silence. 'May their souls be guarded by our ancestors.'

'Now go back to the ranch,' Never-Say-Never said. 'Tell the Phillipses anything you like about the missing cattle, but do not tell them anything about us. We'll be taking one cow a month from now on. You must cover up for us so that your employers do not notice. There are too many cows on this ranch. This is your role in this war. Play it well and you will enjoy the fruits of Independence with the rest of us when it comes. Both of you are now ZIPRA troops. *Salani kahle.*'

Ngwenya and Gumede turned back the way they'd come. But they did not return immediately to the ranch. They slept out, and the following morning Ngwenya reported to Mrs Phillips that they lost the track at the river. He told her they'd spent hours combing the other side, but had found no sign of hoof marks.

From that time, under the careful control of Ngwenya, Wildberg Ranch provided a cow every month to the guerrillas, until, thirty-six cows later, the country gained Independence.

***

Shortly after Mbambo disappeared, news filtered back to the ranch that Mbambo's wives and all their children had also disappeared from their homestead. Apart from clothing and kitchen utensils they had left everything else behind, including all their livestock, which had been taken by the guerrillas. What remained in Mbambo's homestead had been burnt to the ground.

2004

Chapter 21

As soon as Mbambo had appeared on the pavement, Ngwenya had recognised him. After a moment of open-mouthed surprise, he'd risen from his cobbling spot and approached the newcomer, for here was a man from his past.

'It has been a long time Mbambo.' He extended his hand. But Mbambo's face had tightened and he'd turned his attention back to the shoe he was mending, whistling under his breath. Ngwenya stood looking at him, absorbing the unexpected rebuke.

'I do not remember knowing you,' Mbambo finally volunteered without looking up.

'*Hawu* Mbambo! Maybe you're right, so many years have passed, but please let me remind you. I am Samson Ngwenya, you were my foreman at Wildberg Ranch in Plumtree District, and you assisted in having me made the assistant foreman.'

'I do not know of any Wildberg Ranch,' Mbambo retorted. 'If you want to gossip could you please leave me be, as I have some serious work to do.'

Ngwenya gazed at Mbambo in silence. Could he be mistaken? No, he knew this was Mbambo. Sure, he'd changed, he was older, his body was slighter, his hair and moustache had turned grey, but it was undoubtedly Mbambo. Besides, there was that telltale old scar on his forehead. Silently, he returned to his stool under the mango tree.

Ngwenya continued working on his shoes, wondering why Mbambo had rebuked him. He felt more inquisitive than hurt. Was it because of the manner in which he'd left the ranch after the raid? Was he ashamed? Surely, whatever people had done during the war, whether good or bad, was now buried under the sands of time? But Mbambo's rebuke piqued his curiosity – were the rumours about him being a sell-out true? Where had he been all this time?

He'd been certain that Mbambo would quickly be evicted from the shopping centre pavement when Mr Sozinto saw him working there. But not long afterwards, Ngwenya had another surprise. Max, one of the shop assistants, emerged from the supermarket with a shoe and gave it to Mbambo; turning, he caught Ngwenya's eye and shrugged his shoulders as if to say, I have no choice over this. What could be happening? All the workers in the shopping centre gave their shoes to him for repair. And Mbambo had only arrived that very day.

Ngwenya began to observe Mbambo very closely. Within barely a few days, the man behaved as if he owned the pavement. He'd even seen him hobnobbing with Mr Sozinto, like two people who had known each other for a very long time.

'You have serious competition now, Ngwenya,' Max had remarked when he'd come over to Ngwenya for a cigarette break. Max was a young man with carefully styled dreadlocks, and an eye for girls whom he bedded in the back storeroom when Mr Sozinto was not around. Ngwenya knew that while Max was a good-looking young man, he would not have found such easy prey if he wasn't working in a supermarket, especially at a time of shortages.

'Does Mr Sozinto know him?' Ngwenya raised an eyebrow in Mbambo's direction. 'They seem so very friendly.'

'Mr Sozinto told us that he's a distant relative who's just arrived to live in the city.'

'Where from?'

'From the rural areas, a place called something like Cross Jotsholo. Do you know it?'

'Yes, it's a growth point in Lupane District in Matabeleland North.' So that was where Mbambo had been hiding all these years. It made sense. Cross Jotsholo was far enough away from Plumtree if a man wanted to hide.

Chapter 22

Ambition remembered the day that Senzeni had beaten up Power and gotten into serious trouble with their father; not the trouble that had made her run away from home, no, but the incident that had marked the beginning of the problems between his father and his sister. It hadn't been fair. It had been Power who'd started the whole thing.

One day after school, when Ambition and Ntando had taken their wire cars to their racetrack in the bush, they'd found Power and his friend Justin using it. 'Keep moving, boys! Over here,' Power had ordered them, as both Ambition and Ntando hesitated when they'd seen the two older boys, neither of whom was known for their kindness.

'What do you want here?' Power demanded. 'We got here first.'

'But it's our racetrack,' Ambition said.

'What? Don't be silly.' Justin feigned surprise. 'Power and I made this racetrack this afternoon.'

'You're lying,' Ntando flashed. 'Ambition and I made it.'

'Are you calling me a liar?' Power raised his foot. 'You think you're smart, don't you? Well, you don't mess with me!' He brought his foot down hard on Ntando's jeep, and then he turned and kicked Ambition's tipper into the trees. 'Do you really think that you can challenge me?'

Ntando's eyes filled with tears. Only Ambition knew how long it had taken his friend to make his wire jeep. Then Justin stepped forward and slapped Ntando's shaved head.

'Now push off, Bald Head. We don't have time for cry babies here!'

Power laughed, and made ready to slap Ntando again. Without forethought, Ambition leapt at Power, and pushed him hard on the chest with both hands. Power staggered back, grabbing at Ambition's T-shirt. Then his feet had been swept from underneath him as Justin tripped him from behind. As Ambition fell, the two boys had started kicking him. Even with his hands over his ears, as the small boy tried to protect his head, he heard an enraged scream, then the rain of kicks ceased. He got up unsteadily, to see Justin and Power running away, Senzeni after them with a stick. It was not a big stick, but the sound of the blows made it seem bigger. Power tripped and fell down, but Senzeni did not stop hitting him, 'You do not do this to my brother,' she said ferociously as she whacked Power with all her might. Justin turned and fled.

Ambition ran over to Senzeni with Ntando and wrapped his hands around his sister and pulled her away. She appeared possessed and continued screaming. 'You do not beat my brother, you hear! Beat a boy your own size and your own age!'

Breathing deeply, Senzeni calmed down as they all waited for Power to get up. Then Justin, who'd fled, returned with Ambition's father who picked up Power without a word, and carried him back into the township. Just as they arrived, Power came to his senses and demanded to be let down. He said he wanted to go home alone, but Ngwenya insisted that everybody who'd been at the fight must accompany him to MaVundla.

When they arrived, Ngwenya explained to his neighbour, whom they'd found washing clothes, that he'd been summoned by Justin, because 'My daughter was beating your son with a stick.'

'But what had he done to her for Senzeni to do that to him?' MaVundla asked immediately.

'That I do not even want to hear,' his father had replied. 'But what I'm going to do is to teach my daughter a lesson. She must never lay her hands on anybody, and with a stick at that. I'm ashamed and I apologise MaVundla.'

'Please do what you want to do, Ngwenya,' MaVundla dismissed the whole event. 'I have enough troubles of my own and I don't want any children adding to them.' She had poked Power's head with a finger. 'Look at him, in trouble all the time.'

Ambition had opened his mouth to defend Senzeni, but his father had glared at him and told him to shut up. When they'd got home, Ngwenya had broken off a switch from the mulberry tree and whipped Senzeni. He'd made Ambition and Ntando watch, as a lesson to them, so that neither they nor Senzeni should ever lay hands on anybody, no matter what had been done to them.

***

Ambition and Ntando are still watching the Green Bombers at Ilanga Youth Centre. Once they have finished their marching exercises, they are given physical exercises: press-ups, frog-jumps, and sit-ups. The one the two boys like best is when the bombers gyrate their hips as if they are dancing the rumba.

Ntando had laughed the first time he saw this, saying his brother Freedom must try that one too. At that time the youths had not yet been given their uniforms, and had been a rough looking lot. Their looks only improved when they began wearing their green uniform. Now, however, the uniform no longer signalled respectability, but danger. The Green Bombers were disliked and feared in equal measure.

After the physical training session, the youths sit in rows in front of their trainer. 'Now you're going to learn the theory of our beloved Third Chimurenga,' he announces. 'After that you will practise hand-to-hand combat, and then training for today will be over. Today we have a distinguished visitor, a teacher from Lobengula II Primary School, who is going to give us the theory.' The door of the Youth Centre office opened, and ...

'Mrs Gumbo!' Ntando exclaimed.

Dressed in jeans and a T-shirt, the teacher clutched a copy of *From Colonisation to Independence*.

'Clap hands for Mrs Gumbo!' the trainer said, and the Green Bombers applauded.

Chapter 23

Ngwenya pauses and stares in Mbambo's direction. He's not really looking at the other cobbler, but resting his tired hands, which are stiff from sewing through tough fabrics. He flexes his fingers, and peels off rinds of dried glue. His eyes travel slowly across the familiar scene. There's almost no one going in or out of the supermarket because it's easier to find what you want at the flea market where most 'scarce commodities' surface at inflated prices.

He yawns as his eyes flick across the line of vegetable vendors. Almost all of them are selling green *tshomoliya* , and a few have tomatoes and onions as well. There are ten in all, of which only one is a man, somebody from the neighbourhood whose name he doesn't know. For the umpteenth time, Ngwenya wonders how so many vendors selling the same produce can make any money.

He glances at his watch; it's noon. His eyes return to the heap of old shoes at his feet and he sighs. It never seems to grow any less. Then, feeling uncomfortable, he glances in Mbambo's direction and realises that the interloper is now staring at him. As their eyes briefly lock, Mbambo's face twists into something like contempt, before he picks up the bottle of beer he keeps discreetly beside him and takes a long swallow.

Ngwenya shakes his head. Mbambo's antics shouldn't bother him; he considers that perhaps he's paranoid – seeing enemies where there are only friends – the effect of years of hiding from the guerrillas. Suddenly the general midday hum is broken by the shouts of MaVundla' 'Where's my money ,you skelema! I want it right now or I'll show you my true colours!'

'*Futsek*, get away!' Mbambo is undaunted.

'Do you think I'm scared of you? Today I'll expose you. Everyone around here will know that you're a conman who picks up women for sex and then fails to pay them.'

There's a burst of laughter from the vendors.

'Have I ever slept with you? You must be mistaken – you're an old cow.'

'How dare you deny it! You slept with me two weeks back when you repaired my sandal for free, and you promised me Z$2 billion on top! You may have been drunk, indeed you were, but now I want my money!'

***

Ngwenya remembered MaVundla giving her broken sandal to Mbambo. She'd approached him first. She'd been wearing figure-hugging jeans, which Ngwenya thought very inappropriate for older women, let alone women with posteriors the size of MaVundla's.

'No problem, neighbour,' he'd replied, 'but how much are you going to pay me?'

'I haven't any money today,' MaVundla told him, as she chewed her gum. 'Not a single cent, Samson,' calling him by his first name.

Ngwenya inclined his head, 'I'm listening. You're my neighbour, re-member, but my family must also eat.'

'But I'm serious, Samson.' MaVundla had powdered her face and small beads of sweat peeped through the pink sheen. 'I've no money, and I want to go to a party this afternoon and these sandals match my hat.' She preened her body and fluttered her eyelashes. 'Please help me.'

'Your money will help, if you're serious.' Ngwenya smiled. He had a certain respect for this tough lady, but he was immune to her wiles, he'd known her too long.

'I told you, I'm broke.' MaVundla's jaws moved up and down as she chewed, as if the gum was super tough. Her voice dropped to a whisper. 'Come on, you're a man, Samson, and you know I'm alone at home, Thenjiwe will never know.'

Ngwenya shrugged. 'I'm sorry, I don't work that way,' he said carefully. He didn't want to offend her, but who did she think he was?

'Silly ass,' she said, half offended. 'I'm offering you something for free that other people gladly pay for, and you're saying no. You're so slow, that's why you'll die cobbling shoes.' She snatched the offending sandal from his hand and walked away, her large thighs rippling under her jeans.

Ngwenya chuckled as he watched MaVundla walk straight over to Mbambo, who eagerly took her sandal and examined it theatrically, turning it over in his hands as if it was made from some expensive material.

MaVundla blew her gum out saucily and Mbambo nodded his head vigorously; the deal was done.

***

But now the situation was very different. 'If I owe you any money, go to the police right now and make a report!' Mbambo shouted angrily.

'Were the police there when you were on top of me?' Spittle sprays from MaVundla's mouth. 'You bastard!'

'Stupid woman!' Mbambo's eyes search among his tools for a hammer. As he reaches for the handle, MaVundla's foot slams down heavily. Reacting quickly, Mbambo pulls his hand away, and then head butts MaVundla in the stomach. She grabs his T-shirt and pulls hard. It's not a new garment and under the pressure as they strain away from each other, the soft material splits. MaVundla stumbles as it gives and then quickly turns and runs away, bearing aloft Mbambo's torn T-shirt.

Mbambo, his chest heaving, stares at the departing woman. 'I'll have you arrested for defaming the President,' he shouts. 'You cannot tear his face in half and escape. You will go to jail.'

MaVundla pauses and glances at the T-shirt as if she has only just noticed that it once bore the face of the President: 'IDENT, NU PF', glare the remaining letters. 'Just you try, you *mgodoyi!*' she shouts, giving Mbambo the finger.

'I'll get my money from you come hell or shine, you'll see! You think you can intimidate me, but I know your secret, *nja!*' She spits out the last word.

There's loud cheering from the vegetable vendors. One of them calls out, 'Tell us the secret, MaVundla sweetheart!' But MaVundla is already halfway down the street.

Ngwenya wants to laugh, but he contents himself with a chuckle. Street life is better than any play. He wonders what Mbambo's secret can be. Ngwenya can't make the pieces add up. If he betrayed the ZIPRA combatants, and it seems clear that he did, and if he had to flee as a result, which he certainly did, where has he been in the meantime, and how is it that now he seems able to do just as he pleases – and pretends that he knows none of his former colleagues and friends. It all makes no sense.

Ngwenya could go home for lunch now, but he decides to simply take a break and walk around the block. As he passes the open door of the bottle store, he can see Ntando's father, Tshabalala, dancing, a bottle of beer balanced on top of his head, his arms stretched wide in a 'See I'm not holding it' posture. Ngwenya pauses for a moment, and shakes his head sadly: Never-say-Never had been an upright and disciplined cadre, now he was too often just a drunk policeman. And he, too, has changed, Mbambo sighs, thinking back to the young man he once was, full of hope and energy.

Chapter 24

In 1980, when Independence was achieved, everything seemed possible. Zimbabwe became a land of vast opportunity. This was especially so in the cities where even the buildings, the tarred roads and streetlights seemed to reflect the mood of hope and celebration.

Ngwenya and MaNdlovu were amongst the many couples who moved to the city infected by the excitement. When they first arrived, they lived with one of Ngwenya's brothers, Better, who rented two rooms in Makokoba Township. Better also found Ngwenya a job at Perlin Shoes, where he had been working for some time. A year later Better, a bachelor, died from a mysterious illness and Ngwenya and MaNdlovu took on the house and the rent.

Four years later, during those terrible years of Gukurahundi, Ngwenya was promoted to foreman in the shoe factory. As he saved money meticulously, three years later, in 1988, just after the Unity Accord, he'd managed to buy the two-roomed house in Lobengula Township, where they now lived.

They'd met the policeman Tshabalala on the day they arrived in Lobengula. They were offloading their furniture and kitchen utensils when he'd strolled over to watch. Seeing his uniform, Ngwenya had been alarmed, for stories were rife of people being conned into bad housing deals. Then the policeman, a glass of beer in hand, had politely greeted them, and introduced himself.

'My name is Tshabalala. I'm your neighbour,' he said, using the glass to indicate the house to the left. 'I was just about to take off my uniform when I saw you through the window and I thought you could use a hand, seeing that our madam here is heavy with child.'

Ngwenya was glad to accept his offer. 'Ah, good then,' Tshabalala went on, in a friendly fashion. 'I was wondering when the new owners would arrive – it's not good for a house to remain empty, otherwise goblins might move in and make it their base of operations.'

They'd all laughed and Tshabalala put down his beer and helped Ngwenya to carry in all the remaining furniture. As he did so he chatted as if they were old friends, and indeed there did seem something oddly familiar about him. He told them that he had a wife, and a son, Freeman, who were currently visiting his wife's mother.

When they'd finished, the two men stood at the gate exchanging a little of their life histories. Suddenly, the new neighbour stopped Ngwenya mid-flow, 'Did you say Wildberg Ranch? That's why you seem familiar. You're Foreman Ngwenya. We met on a couple of occasions,' and he stuck out his hand, 'Never-Say-Never!'

***

Tshabalala, still balancing the beer on his head, removes one of his shoes. His audience clap their hands and whistle; someone yells 'Never-Say-Never!' and bursts out laughing. Tshabalala puts on the shoe again, removes the bottle from his head and bows; then he walks towards the door of bottle store, a big drunken smile on his face.

Seeing Ngwenya, he stops and stares at him, as if he is trying to remember something. His smile has been replaced by a careful expression. Suddenly, he turns round, and lurches toward Mbambo, who always has a liquid lunch, and after his confrontation with MaVundla quickly sought solace with a beer. Tshabalala slaps Mbambo on the back, says something, and the two men laugh. Ngwenya has never seen them laughing together like this before.

In fact, if he recalls correctly, they rarely ever speak to each other; they'd been on opposite sides during the war, after all. To do him justice, Tshabalala had made overtures toward Mbambo when he'd first arrived, but Mbambo had denied knowing him, denied ever being at the ranch, and as Tshabalala confided to Ngwenya one evening, 'I can't abide a liar.'

But here they were, talking and laughing. 'Never-Say-Never!' Mbambo shouts raising his beer. 'Never-Say-Never!' Tshabalala echoes. 'Cheers!' And they clink bottles.

Ngwenya is hurt. He's known the policeman a long time; after all, he helped him with thirty-four head of cattle, and here he was shunning him and preferring to laugh with that sell-out. He turns to go back to his stall, his heart heavy, and as he does so, Mbambo brushes past him, not returning to his place on the pavement, but moving fast in the direction of the northern suburbs.

Ngwenya settles back on his stool, sighs and starts stitching. He suddenly knows why Tshabalala has shunned him. It's because he and his family did not reply to his greeting when they were on their way to exorcise Ambition's strange pieces of cloth. Unbidden, a laugh wells up – just my luck, he thinks, I consult an *inyanga*, and become enemies with a neighbour, and a good one, too!

But the *inyanga* had had to be consulted, and not only because of his child's health. The whole spiritual existence of his family had been at stake. Had he replied to Tshabalala's greeting, there'd have been no reason to go to the bush.

Surely it had not always been like this? Surely there'd been a time when small disagreements and misunderstandings had been settled with a laugh, a handshake, or over a glass of beer. What was happening? Was it politics or poverty or both? If they'd been able to overcome their differences after the war, how could it be that everyone was so divided now? And yet Mbambo had deliberately rejected his overtures, deliberately set up as a rival in the shoe-repairing business and at a time when every cent counted. And then there'd been that business with MaNdlovu's stolen petticoat. That the story had made the rounds, and that he'd become a laughing stock, was entirely due to Mbambo.

Inevitably, it had happened at the bottle store. Everyone had been very drunk, among them the criminal Bra Ngeja. Mbambo had been in a funny mood, sitting by his shoes, not working, but drinking, and occasionally going into the store for another bottle of beer. 'Where did he ever get the money from?' Ngwenya thought, behind his own pile of worn and broken shoes.

And then all of a sudden Mbambo had come out of the store, beer in hand, followed by a group of drunken men hooting with laughter, and his rival had pointed at him, and laughed uproariously. It had been most unpleasant and after a few moments of allowing himself to be the butt of some joke, Ngwenya had had enough. He got up and walked over to the bottle store. As he entered the dim interior, howls of laughter filled the room above the loud music blasting from a hi-fi, and BraNgeja had shouted, 'What's she wearing now, Papa?

'Mbambo says he saw your daughter Senzeni selling a petticoat and pair of new red knickers at the beer garden this morning!' Bra Ngeja slapped his hands together. 'And when he asked where she'd got them from, she told him they were her mother's, but they were new and she was selling them to make money!'

Ngwenya didn't wait to hear more. He was mortified with shame and confusion, and although it was a long time before he usually knocked off, he immediately collected his cobbling equipment and cycled home.

True, his wife had spent the whole of the previous day looking for her new underwear, which she said had disappeared from the wardrobe. She'd suspected witchcraft; new undergarments could be used to make a woman menstruate until she died from loss of blood. Alternatively, if someone wanted to put a spell on her, all they needed was a petticoat or a pair of knickers, so MaNdlovu was very worried.

Senzeni had not been home when he arrived, so he'd had the rest of the afternoon to seethe over his humiliation. It was more than he could bear that people thought he did not make enough money, and reduced the women in his family to selling their underclothes. He barely spoke to MaNdlovu, telling her only that he was very, very angry with their daughter.

Late that evening, when Senzeni eventually arrived, Ngwenya wasted no time. After closing and locking the door, he had grabbed Senzeni from behind and commanded his wife to search her. MaNdlovu had done so, and found the missing pair of panties in the back pocket of her jeans; the petticoat was missing.

'How could you do this Senzeni?' Ngwenya had shouted, beside himself with rage.

'You know nothing,' Senzeni retaliated in a mixture of anger and fear. 'You just *hate* me!'

Ngwenya let go of her to grab a stick from behind the cupboard, but Senzeni had been too fast for him. She leapt across the small room and through the open window.

'You'll see one day! I'll show you!' Senzeni shouted back into the house.

Chapter 25

At Ilanga Youth Centre, Ambition's eyes are fixed on Mrs Gumbo.

'What's she doing there?' Ntando asks, alarmed, as if he wants to shout a warning.

'They'll beat her up if she doesn't watch out!'

'I don't think they'll do that,' Ambition says, for he's noticed that Mrs Gumbo is wearing a white T-shirt bearing the head of the President, just like the one worn by the Green Bombers. Indeed, the Bombers stand up when they see Mrs Gumbo.

'Good afternoon, Mrs Gumbo,' Ntando says involuntarily, as if he too were in the class.

'Good afternoon boys and girls,' Mrs Gumbo says. She's smiling, something she rarely does at school, 'And how are you today?'

'Fine, thanks, and how are you?' Ntando knows the drill by heart, as the young people on parade clearly do.

'Fine, you may sit down now,' Mrs Gumbo tells the Green Bombers, and both Ntando and Ambition sit down as well.

The leader of the Green Bombers offers Mrs Gumbo a chair and she sits down and proceeds to read from her history textbook, which provides all the names of black leaders who were involved in the war of liberation, as well as those of the ministers since 1980. These are facts, which they are supposed to learn by heart. Afterwards they have to learn the names of all the minerals found in the country. And at the end of every lesson Mrs Gumbo explains how white people made black people slaves and that whites are very evil people.

'When white people came to Africa, they had nothing and we had everything. But look around you now, they have everything, and we have nothing. Do you think that's good?'

'No!' the Green Bombers yell, 'Down with white people.'

'Look at all the black people who run away to Europe, thinking they're going to find good jobs there. What are they doing now? The white people refuse to give them good jobs because, like I told you, they regard them as baboons. So they make them their slaves and force them to do their dirty jobs. But what do we do here in Zimbabwe when we see a white person? We want to grovel at their feet and worship them! Where is our pride as black people? What happened to the dream of Dr Martin Luther King please tell me?'

'Who is Doctor Martin?' Ntando whispers.

'Maybe he's a doctor in town that Mrs Gumbo visits when she's not feeling well. He's probably a white person, because his name is "King".'

'Now I'm going to read an excerpt from Dr Martin Luther King's speech. "I have a dream that one day even the state of Mississippi, a state sweltering with the heat of injustice, sweltering with the heat of oppression, will be transformed into an oasis of freedom and justice ..."'

'Her doctor is very good in English,' Ntando comments. 'What's Mississippi?'

'Maybe it's an injection for *mararia*, but shhh, let's listen.'

Mrs Gumbo folds away Dr Martin Luther King's dream, and puts the piece of paper back inside the textbook.

'But how can our Mississippi be transformed into an oasis of freedom and justice when white people continue sabotaging us every day?'

'Mississipi must be a country,' Ambition says.

'There are even some of our own black people who have joined the white people in trying to reverse the little gains of our Independence,' Mrs Gumbo continues, 'which we lost blood for during the war of liberation. Just look at M.D.C.' She provides an emphatic pause between each letter. 'What are they trying to do? Mhh?'

'Down with the MDC!' the Green Bombers shout.

'I'll tell you a story,' Mrs Gumbo's voice assumes a gossipy tone. 'One day last year during the athletics competitions at my school, something happened that nearly drove me to doing something I did not think I could do...'

Mrs Gumbo pauses for effect, and looks at the seated youths. 'I was one of the recorders of the running events; sitting next to me was that man Nkani, who's now campaigning to be an MP for the MDC, the traitors.'

The Green Bombers have obviously heard this story before, and they start whistling and chanting: 'Down with Mr Nkani! Down with Mr Nkani!'

The trainer raises his hand, and the noise dies down.

Mrs Gumbo squares her shoulders and continues. 'During the hundred metre race, the girl who was coming second tripped the girl who was about to win, and do you know what happened?'

'No!' The Green Bombers say with one voice, though they do.

'Mr Nkani shouted "Hey, don't behave like the President!"' Mrs Gumbo puts her hand on her chest. 'You know, I felt pain in my heart, and I couldn't help myself. Please God forgive me, I gave him a punch right in the face.' She punches the air in front of her. 'What could he do,' she laughs. 'A man must not strike a woman; anyway, his body is almost as thin as my arm.' Her voice drops to a whisper, 'I don't know about his penis.'

The Green Bombers burst into wild laughter.

The trainer raises his hand and the Green Bombers fall quiet. Mrs Gumbo continues. 'And then he made a mistake, he threw a slap at my face. So I gave him another one right here.' She points at her throat. 'I heard him grunt like a pig. I knew he was now mine.' Mrs Gumbo is now feinting, just like a boxer on TV when he's warming up. 'He tried to throw a jab at my face, but I ducked.' She ducks. 'Then I saw that he was wide open, and I swung an uppercut at his chin.' She swings a right uppercut. 'And do you know what happened next?'

'No!' the bombers chorus on cue.

'But first, I'll tell you a secret that most people don't know.' She pauses. 'If I tell you, please don't repeat it.' MaGumbo says again, 'it's top secret.

'Most people know that I am a full war veteran, not so?'

'Yes,' the Green Bombers chorus. 'You helped to save our country!' Mrs Gumbo raises her hand, part acknowledgment, part a request for silence.

'But I'm also an undercover agent for the police.' Her voice drops. 'I don't work for the CIO, I report straight to the Chief of Police about any nonsense that happens in my school, or anything that threatens the security of our great nation.'

The Green Bombers burst into applause, clapping their hands, and whistling.

'She's a spy!' Ambition whispers.

'My father is a war veteran and a policeman, too,' Ntando says.

Mrs Gumbo clears her throat. 'You don't mess with me! So, when I hit that Mr Nkala, he turned and fled, just imagine!' She laughs merrily and claps her hands.

The Green Bombers cheer with good spirit.

'But, do you think that I, a war veteran, would leave it there? No. No, I chased him.'

'Power was lying when he said Mrs Gumbo beat Mr Nkani because he saw her in the toilet,' Ntando tells Ambition.

'Down with puppets!' Mrs Gumbo shouts. '*Phansi labo!*'

The Green Bombers punch their fists into the air. 'Down with them!'

'*Viva!*'

'*Viva!*' the bombers chant.

There's a pause. Mrs Gumbo turns to the trainer, who's been standing beside her and they shake hands. Mrs Gumbo then turns back to the Green Bombers.

'Okay comrades, I'll see you in two days for the next Third Chimurenga theory lesson. *Viva*'

'*Viva!*'

Mrs Gumbo turns and walks towards the gate.

'All rise,' the trainer shouts, 'I am now handing you over to Comrade Tshisa.'

The man in green overalls and a black balaclava appears.

Ambition and Ntando know that it's long been time to go home but they can't drag themselves away from the fence and the next episode in the drama.

Chapter 26

It's the not the first time that Ambition and Ntando have seen Comrade Tshisa, who always wears a face mask, which fascinates them. They had once asked Senzeni why he hid his face, and Senzeni had told them it was none of their business. But the arrival of the man in the balaclava reminds them that their ostensible reason for being there was to see Senzeni, and they are going to get into trouble for being away so long.

'Senzeni must come now to us,' Ntando says 'We've been waiting for too long.' Their eyes rake the Green Bombers and they find Senzeni, who looks over towards them. The two boys wave frantically but she motions them to wait.

The Green Bombers begin training again under the instruction of Comrade Tshisa. As usual, under his watch, they are instructed how to beat people up with a mixture of fist fighting, stone throwing and so-called karate. Mostly they just flail their arms and grunt.

***

The second time Senzeni beat a child happened at school, just a few months after she'd beaten up Power. Ironically, Ambition had heard about it from Power, when he had been playing slug with Ntando at the shopping centre near their school. When Power arrived, he said without preliminaries, 'Your sister is crazy!'

'If you say that again I'll tell her, and you know what will happen to you.'

'I could have beaten her up that day in the bush,' Power said defensively. 'But she's possessed! If she doesn't watch it, one day she'll kill somebody and go to jail.'

'It's you who's mad,' Ambition retaliated. 'If it wasn't for the likes of you, my sister would be having a good reputation.'

'Nxa,' Power clicked his tongue. 'Today at school she seriously beat up a girl called Pretty. Right now she's serving punishment digging a very deep hole. Do you know why she beat her up?'

'I don't want to know,' Ambition said. 'Senzeni doesn't beat anyone up without a reason.'

'Tell us,' interjected Ntando, and Power, who couldn't really wait to tell the story, responded.

'Because Pretty laughed at her, saying that her father is just a shoe cobbler. Your father was called to the school by the headmaster for it. Tell me, boys, would anybody with their senses intact attack another person just for that?'

'But you go around beating up litte boys who can't defend themselves,' Ambition said, and Ntando added, 'I would beat anybody who laughed at my father and said he drinks too much.'

'Nxa, you're all crazy,' Power muttered, knowing that he couldn't hit either of them with so many people around.

That night when Ambition's father had come from work, he had whipped Senzeni again, telling her that he had told her time and time again never to beat up other children. Senzeni had cried a lot and gone into the bedroom.

***

Finally, after some stone throwing, the training session comes to an end, and as the Green Bombers head for the building of the Youth Centre, Ambition sees Senzeni walking quickly towards them.

'What do you want now?' she asks when she reaches them. She sounds exasperated. 'Isn't it that you were here a few hours ago?'

Ntando lifts the scoff tin. 'Are you still hungry?'

'What's that?'

'Mother said we should bring you food.'

Senzeni casts a quick look behind her, and then bends down, grips the bottom strand of barbed wire and pulls it up.

'Push the tin under,' she says. Ntando quickly does so. Ambition pushes the bag with the T-shirt through the gap as well.

Senzeni lets the wire go.

'What's in the plastic bag?'

'It's the T-shirt we brought earlier. I thought I should bring it back. You'll need it, Senzeni.'

'You really are insistent aren't you?' There's a glint of a smile in her eyes. She glances behind her again, takes the plastic bag, and shoves it down the front of her trousers under her T-shirt.

'Do you have muscles now, Senzeni?' Ntando flexes the bicep of his right arm. 'We saw you doing press-ups.'

'Stop making noise and go back home.' Senzeni won't be drawn.

Ambition is looking at the Green Bombers, who are massed in front of the centre. Comrade Tshisa is standing in the shade of the building, and the trainer is giving the Green Bombers bottles out of a cardboard box. Ambition recognises them as hotstuff. Then the trainer raises his hands.

'Okay comrades,' he says loudly. 'Today's training is over.' He turns to Tshisa. 'Thank you Comrade Tshisa, that was a very good workout.' The two men shake hands.

'The youths need to be strong,' Comrade Tshisa says. 'The other day I saw people in the township chasing them, and when they arrived back here, I gave them all two very hard claps. This is not a ballroom dancing club.'

'You did good.'

Comrade Tshisa flexes his arm. 'We must concentrate on teaching them how to throw stones harder. You must buy them weights, they need to strengthen their muscles.'

'You're right, Comrade Tshisa, I'll have that sorted soon.'

'It takes time, but eventually they'll become what we want them to become. See you tomorrow.' And the two men salute each other.

***

Ambition's eyes follow Comrades Tshisa. His overalls are baggy and flap around his legs. He heads for a hole in the fence, avoiding the main gate, which Ambition thinks is a very strange thing to do. He's not a big man and he's agile, so he bends down to push himself through.

But when he puts his head down, the mask snags on the barbed wire, and the balaclava comes off. Ambition's jaw drops. It is 3Pac. Mbambo snatches the mask, puts it back and disappears into the bush.

'What is it, Ambition?' Senzeni turns round and asks her brother, who's staring at the fence with a strange expression on his face.

'Nothing.' He lifts his hand and touches Senzeni's fingers.

'Bye-bye, Senzeni, we're going home now.'

'See you next time, Ambi, and you too Ntando.'

Ntando gives the raised thumb salute.

Chapter 27

The following morning, Ambition left home soon after breakfast, and after his mother had gone to hawk her vegetables around the streets. His father had left even earlier, explaining that there was a customer who wanted to collect his shoes before he went to work.

Ambition is walking fast down the path he'd walked with his parents when they'd gone for the cleansing ceremony. He has passed the boulders and the cluster of thorn trees and not met anyone, but he can hear the *amapostori* singing somewhere to his left. He finally comes to the fork. Crickets are trilling and a pin-sized aeroplane sparkles as it crosses the blue sky, heading north and leaving a smoky white contrail.

He sighs with relief: the cloth pieces are just where they'd left them with the plastic container. Ambition picks them up. He wraps the strip of red cloth inside the larger piece of white material, and stuffs the small bundle inside his jogger shorts, just as Senzeni had done with her T-shirt the day before.

'It's not working,' he says in a small voice, an image of Senzeni carrying the flag and marching with the Green Bombers flashing across his mind. 'She doesn't want to come home.' He pauses for a moment, then turns to go back to the township.

As he passes the boulders, he sees a movement. He stops, poised for instant flight should the need arise. A thin youth in a green T-shirt and sun hat is darting from rock to rock, as if stalking something, or as if he's being followed. Ambition is intrigued and can't help following behind in his own game of cops and robbers. Finally, the youth pauses behind a big rock, and peers behind him. To his astonishment, he sees that the youth is Senzeni. Ambition does not call out. Something tells him that she would be very angry.

A part of Ambition's mind tells him that maybe Senzeni is skulking for hidden lovers, a game they used to play. But he knows this is wishful thinking; Senzeni would never leave the Green Bombers to come and play a childish game.

Senzeni is wholly absorbed and quite unaware of being followed. She's staring at something beyond her and she doesn't want to be seen. Ambition creeps forward. A twig cracks under his foot, but Senzeni has not heard him, and he moves forward. Suddenly he can see what she's looking at: beneath a large tree, a group of women is assembled. They're all sitting on the ground, looking at the woman who is addressing them. It's Mrs Nkani. She is sitting on a big stone and on her lap is a counter book with a hard black cover.

A woman rises and moves toward Mrs Nkani. Ambition's heart jumps and for a moment he feels faint with surprise – it's his mother! She says something and gives the leader or secretary or whoever she is, something that looks like money. Mrs Nkani accepts it, and writes something down in her book. Then she reaches into a bag at her side, produces a card and hands it to his mother, who quickly slips it into her bra.

Then Mrs Nkani reaches into her bag again, takes out a stack of papers and hands these to his mother, who puts them in a plastic bag and returns to the group of women.

Mrs Nkani stands up. 'We women carry the hopes of our families in our hands,' she says in a strong voice. 'Our husbands, if they've not fled to the diaspora, to South Africa, or Botswana, are busy at work. They're trying to earn a living, so that our children can eat, and in a country where people with ruling party backing are looting everything in sight.' She points a finger at MaNdlovu. 'Thank you for finally joining us MaNdlovu, we now understand the problem with your daughter as you've just explained it to us this morning. We know she's a good girl but her mind has been poisoned by the militia and there's nothing anyone can do about that for now. But always remember that we are behind you. We will never blame you for the deeds of others, even if they are of your blood. I was wrong that night when my home was petrol-bombed by the militia. I should not have blamed you for that.'

Ambition looks towards Senzeni, who is writing furiously in a notebook, pausing now and then to look at the gathering. He wonders what she can be writing and who will be able read it, as Senzeni has bad handwriting and grammar.

'Please, I ask you to exercise extreme caution these days,' Mrs Nkani continues. 'You all know what we're faced with out there in the streets.'

A lizard darts to the top of the rock and stops, barely a breath away from Ambition's face; it raises its head and stares at him through small glittering eyes, like glass beads.

'Go away,' Ambition hisses, and bends down to pick up a small stone from the ground.

As he does so his feet slip and a small avalanche of pebbles slide down between the boulders. Ambition holds himself completely still, aware that he's made a lot of noise, but the women have all disappeared.

He looks anxiously in Senzeni's direction and realises that she's seen him. Ambition can feel the rage that fills her. The silence between them is broken by a third presence, who emerges from behind Senzeni, Mr Nkani. A gust of wind blows across the dry veld, leaves rustle, and the whistle of a train blows faintly in the distance.

'Come here right now, Ambition!' Senzeni shouts, her voice unexpectedly loud in the stillness. At that moment, Mr Nkani reaches over her shoulder and grabs the note book from her hand. Senzeni twists around to hit him, but he ducks. Senzini loses her balance and Mr Nkani vanishes behind the rock.

Ambition feels utterly confused by this chain of events. He wants to go over to his sister to check that she's all right, but he's sure she'll only shout at him. Maybe she'll even accuse him of leading Mr Nkani to her hiding place. He feels awash with anxiety and a strange excitement. 'I need to go home,' he thinks.

Chapter 28

He emerges into Emakhandeni Township behind the Power Station and walks past it. He crosses Luveve road, and walks beside Njube Hill. The top of the hill is filled with small groups of *amapostori* worshippers chanting their prayers to the sky.

He crosses Masiyephambili Road, enters Lobengula Township and spots his mother walking away from him. A dish of vegetables is balanced on her head. She calls out in a thin and detached voice, 'Cheap vegetables! Cheap vegetables for sale!'

'Mama!' Ambition runs in her direction. Pages of red paper are strewn all over the ground behind her. MaNdlovu stops and turns. Sweat is dripping down her face, and a frown creases her brow.

'Where are you coming from?' she asks anxiously. She looks worried, and she takes his hand and leads him into the shade of a guava tree.

'From... from... ' Ambition pauses, relieved; she wouldn't ask the question if she'd seen him hiding behind the boulder.

'Stop stammering, Ambi. You mustn't play far away from home. Haven't I told you that there are people who steal stubborn children like you?'

'Okay, Mama.' Ambition bends down and picks up a stray piece of the red papers.

'Put that down at once!'

Ambition drops the paper. He gazes at the blue plastic bag that his mother is holding, a scroll of paper peeping out of the top.

'What are you staring at?' she asks, tucking the bag under her arm as if she doesn't want him to see what's in it. 'Go home at once.'

'Yes, Mama.' Ambition grins. 'And please bring me some sweets when you come home.'

MaNdlovu's careworn face breaks into a smile. 'Yes I will, my son.' She pats his shoulder. 'You know I love you. Please go home now.'

MaNdlovu continues up the street. 'Cheap vegetables for sale! Cheap vegetables for sale!'

Ambition watches her for a moment, and sees his mother's hand reach into her bag, pull out the scroll of paper, and release the rubber band to let the pages float behind her as if she's performed a magical feat. Then she turns a corner and disappears.

A few streets further along, Ambition comes upon a group of children, all younger than him. He recognises them but does not know most of them by name. They're milling excitedly around a ditch miming expressions of horror.

'What is it?' Ambition asks, as he peers into the ditch.

Ntando's father lies upside down, his head slightly tilted, snoring noisily. One hand clutches a cellphone.

'What's wrong with him?'

'He was peeing into the ditch,' answers a boy in a bright blue cap. 'Then he did this...' The boy teeters on the edge of the ditch milling his arms as if he'd lost his balance.

'And he fell inside!' a girl adds, and all the children burst out laughing.

'He's very drunk!' another boy exclaims. 'I saw him at the bottle store this morning dancing with a bottle of beer on his head like this!' He places a fist on his head and wiggles his hips. 'Never-Say-Never!' The boy calls out, to more laughter.

Ambition climbs down into the ditch, and shakes Tshabalala by the shoulder.

'Hey, wake up, saNtando!'

Tshabalala reeks of alcohol and cigarettes, and does not respond.

'Let's look for water and pour it over him,' the boy with the blue cap advises. 'My father did that to my mother once when she came home drunk from a party!'

'This is a policeman,' Ambition says. 'And if you do that to him and he wakes up you will all rot in jail!'

One of the children inhales sharply in mock horror. 'We're all so frightened,' she says, and they all laugh.

Ambition shakes Tshabalala again. This time he swats Ambition's hand and mutters, 'I can't beat my neighbours, even if it's for the Party, please Inspector.' His voice is slurred. 'This...er ishn't why we...er wernt to war.'

'*Hai ah!* He can't beat us when he's so drunk. Listen to him!' The children howl with merriment.

Tshabalala wriggles into a more comfortable position, snoring loudly and rhythmically.

Ambition extricates the cellphone from his hand and climbs out of the ditch. 'Look after him, okay guys? I'm going to tell Freeman and Ntando what's happened and they'll come and collect him. If he wakes up and asks for his cellphone, tell him I took it. Is there anybody here who does not know me?'

'Senzeni's young brother,' a girl's voice pipes up. 'That girl who set fire to Mr Nkani's house.'

'Shut up Sylvia!'

'I heard MaVundla telling my mother that, Bheki!' the girl protests. 'Senzeni is now a Green Bomber. And you shut up too, you're not my father!'

***

MaChivanda's home is the biggest and most modern in her line, now that she's renovated it. Like all the others it had once been just a simple two-roomed house with a *delele* hedge, but the sudden boom in the money-changing business had made her family rich. Her house is painted a bright yellow and has red roof tiles. The hedge has been replaced with a cheap durawall, which soon began to collapse, so Mai Chivanda is now replacing it with grey breezeblock wall. Progress is slow, bcause cement is scarce.

Ambition walks through a partly open gate, Tshabalala's cellphone in his hand, his mission to find Freeman and Ntando temporarily suspended. He walks across Mai Chivanda's clean new paving toward the back of the house and the kitchen. Peering through the half-curtained window he can see a big bundle of dollar notes on the kitchen table. He allows himself a minute to gawk at the four-plate stove, big refrigerator, and dresser laden with cups and saucers, when he hears a man saying goodbye. He instantly recognises Bra Ngeja's voice.

'See you next time, Bra Ngeja,' MaChivanda replies. 'Remember to tell all your relatives and friends to change their forex with me. I'll give you a comission on everyone you send.'

'Don't worry, MaChivanda. I know a lot of people who change their money in town and come back crying when they find they've been conned. We can do good business together.'

Ambition freezes. He had not expected to see or hear anyone. He knows that MaChivanda is afraid of being robbed, and always locks herself inside the house while waiting for customers.

MaChivanda laughs. 'We tell people to come to me, but they think they will just be making me rich. Let them go to town, Bra Ngeja; when they've learnt their lesson they'll come crawling back.'

Bra Ngeja appears in the backyard. He's carrying a plastic bag bulging with bundles of Zim dollar notes. Ambition steps to the side to let him pass, but Bra Ngeja blocks his his way.

'Aha, caught you! What are you doing, small boy. Spying, eh?' He's dressed in a white knee-length Nigerian shirt, black trousers and a cap. A cellphone dangles on his chest from a strap around his neck.

'What did I do?' Ambition asks.

'What did you say that day when you were with your mother?' Bra Ngeja snaps. 'Heh? Do you know my boy, I could even kill you and nobody can touch me?' He wags his finger.

Ambition knows he should be afraid, but for some reason he's not. He doesn't think that Bra Ngeja will put down all that money in order to beat him. He also can't really believe that someone like Bra Ngeja really cares what insults Ambition throws at him. If Bra Ngeja is the elephant, Ambition knows he's the flea.

'But talking with poor shit like you is a waste of time.' He waves his bag in front of Ambition's nose. 'Has your father ever had so much money, *mfana*? Has he?'

Ambition retains his cool, and says nothing. He reckons silence is his best defence, and it will infuriate Bra Ngeja.

'Tell your father to cobble shoes harder, my boy,' on the man continues. 'Maybe one day he'll be able to buy his family more than a loaf of bread.' He laughs, and steps around Ambition, the bag of money swinging in his hand. 'And take care that cellphone doesn't walk away from you.'

Ambition stares at Bra Ngeja's back for a moment, peeps back through the kitchen window to assure himself that Mai Chivanda has taken no notice, then continues to the back door, where he quickly removes the small bundle of cloth from his crotch and places it on the doorstep. As he does so Tshabalala's cellphone begins to ring. He looks at it in confusion, for he's never used a cellphone. Then the back door swings open.

MaChivanda, resplendent in her customary white gown stares down at him in surprise. 'So, you've bought a cellphone, Ambi?' She smiles, as a mouth-watering aroma of fried chicken wafts through the door.

'It belongs to Ntando's father.'

'Answer it then,' MaChivanda says, then clears her throat, and shouts, 'Sisi, please don't burn that chicken! Some people are starving and you're burning good meat!' She turns back to Ambition.

'Answer it, Ambition.'

'I don't know how to.'

'Then why did that policeman give it to you? Give it to me.' She takes the cellphone, depresses a button and puts it to her ear.

'Hello? ... I'm sorry this is not Mr Tshabalala but a neighbour. ... Yes, I am a woman ... No, I have a cold.' She coughs to clear her throat. 'Oh, you're the police. I'm sorry this phone is with a neighbour's child, but I'm sure if you phone later, you'll get Tshabalala. ... A message? Yes I can pass it on to him. ... Today, as soon as he can? Yes, yes, I'll pass it on. Thank you.'

She cuts the call and looks at Ambition. 'Oh God, my voice, too much singing last night at church. Bless the Lord. Where is Never-Say-Never?'

'He's sleeping in a ditch. I took his cellphone so that thieves won't steal it. I can take you to him. Maybe you can carry him home. He's very heavy.'

MaChivanda grimaces. 'No thank you. I'm a church person, you know that. Go and tell his boy Freeman and also tell him that Never-Say-Never is wanted at work right now by his Inspector.' She hands the phone back. 'And make sure you don't lose this cellphone, Ambi, otherwise it might get you into big big trouble.' She leans over and pinches his right cheek.

'I won't lose it.' Ambition turns to walk away.

'Hey. Stop,' MaChivanda calls. She held up the white cloth and the strip of red material that Ambition had placed on the door step. 'I see you've brought our priest's property back.'

'Yes.' he replies in a small voice.

'Very good.' MaChivanda smiles at him. 'The priest's been asking for you. Will you come tomorrow? Last time you ran away! What kind of a man will you grow up to be? You mustn't be afraid of our priest, sweetheart, he doesn't wish harm on anybody. Worshipping the Lord is a good thing...' MaChivanda begins to cough, waves at Ambition, steps back into her house and closes the door.

Chapter 29

When he reaches the half-built wall at the back of MaChivanda's home, he climbs onto the refuse bin beside it and, holding Tshabalala's cellphone tightly, leaps over. Pigeons explode from in front of him as he lands in his own yard. He walks past the *tshomoliya* vegetable patch to the back door and tries it. It's locked. That means his mother is not yet back.

He debates removing the key from underneath the doormat, but decides against it. Instead, he places the cellphone in the back pocket of his shorts, and walks to the hole in the hedge that leads to Ntando's home. Freeman is standing at his back door looking in Ambition's direction. A thin trail of smoke rises from his hand. He beckons the boy over. Ntando is sitting beside his brother with a long length of wire which he is attempting to bend into a shape.

Ambition squeezes through the hole, and walks over to them. 'I saw you peeping at me through the window yesterday morning,' Freeman says in an accusing voice. 'Why are you and Ntando like that?' He's wearing a white T-shirt decorated with a large green marijuana leaf on the chest, and his dreadlocks fall to his shoulders.

Ambition is embarrassed, and kicks at some loose soil.

'You and Ntando really messed up my game plan.' He takes a puff of his joint, and expels smoke in a tight stream. 'Nobuhle immediately said no after I'd seen you peeping through the curtain. She's now very angry with me and says I wanted to cheat her into something she didn't want to do.'

Ambition smiles. He hadn't wanted anything to happen to Nobuhle.

'What are you smiling at? I've told Ntando he will grow boils in his eyes if he continues to peep at me, but will he listen – just look at him!' He glares at Ntando, whose concentrates on the wire he's moulding. Then, unexpectedly, Freeman explodes into laughter.

'You're so funny!' He has a deep and pleasant laugh. He takes a puff of his joint. 'I don't know what I should call you,' he says between coughs. 'The two ma-peepers?' He shouts with laughter at his own joke and Ntando and Ambition begin to laugh as well. Freeman squats down to Ambition's height. He drags on his joint, and blows the smoke over Ambition's head. 'Do you know how to propose love to a girl, my dear boy?'

'I don't do that, I'm still a child.'

Freeman squints at Ambition, his eyes glittering brightly. 'At your age I was kissing girls, but you young boys haven't an ounce of romance in you. What's the matter with you? Don't you know that girls will laugh at you and look down on you, because they want it from you?'

Ambition opens his mouth to reply, and then jumps back as the cellphone rings. He takes it out of his pocket and offers it to Freeman, who raises his eyebrows.

'Take it. It belongs to your father.'

'Never-Say-Never's cellphone?' Tendrils of smoke drift from Freeman's nostrils. 'Where did you get it from?' He takes the cellphone. 'Hello. No, this is not Mr Tshabalala, but his son. Hold on.' He covers its mouthpiece. 'Where is the Sergeant?' he whispers.

'He's lying in a ditch near the shops. If we go now I'll show you where he is.'

'He's drunk!' Freeman declares, and straightens up.

'Hello? Please phone later, my father has just gone to visit our uncle who's not feeling well and he left his cellphone behind. ... Okay, I'll tell him Inspector. Goodbye.' He puts the phone in his pocket.

'Where did you say you saw papa, Ambi?' Ntando asks.

'He's sleeping in a ditch by the shops.'

'Lord Jesus, he's wanted at work to police the streets of our city, and what's he doing? Sleeping in a ditch! Okay, let's go and fetch the Sergeant, boys. We can't afford to have a father who's the township clown, can we? And all because of mother's British pounds!' He reflects for a moment. 'We'd better take the wheelbarrow with us. We'll look like fools, but we'll never be able to carry him by ourselves if he's drunk.

***

They find an empty bottle in the ditch.

'He was lying next to that bottle,' Ambition says, pointing at the indentation in the ground.

'His water!' Freeman shrugs dismissively.

There's nobody to be seen, the children have all gone.

'I'm sure he's gone back to Easy Way,' Ntando grins. 'Maybe he's balancing a bottle on his head right now. Let's go and watch, guys.'

Freeman looks at Ntando. 'Maybe you're right – for once in your life! Let's cut across there now, guys.'

They walk up the street. Freeman pushes the wheelbarrow. The sun has begun to set, casting long fingers of shadow down the road.

They turn into a street that leads to the shops, which is crowded with people, as if everyone has come out of their houses to relish the last minutes of the setting sun and the cool of the evening.

'Ambition, listen to me,' Freeman says. 'I want to send you to that girl.'

'Which girl?'

'The one who ran away from me yesterday,' Freeman laughs. 'Who else do you think? I only have one girlfriend in the township, you know that. '

'I'm afraid of my father.' Ambition does not want to run errands for Freeman.

'You won't have to go into her home. You'll just stand in your yard under the mulberry tree, and when she comes out of the door, slip her this over the fence.' Freeman takes an envelope from his pocket and gives it to Ambition.

'But what if I'm caught?'

'This is a free lesson for the future, my boy, from a language student at university; it's a lesson you'll never learn in any school.'

'I'm changing school next year,' Ntando intervenes. 'I'm going to learn in town. I don't like the township schools. Later when I grow up I'll go to university like you, Freeman.'

'Shut up, Ntando, you won't go to a town school, you're too mischievous,' Freeman tells his brother. 'And you'll only get lost on the way.'

'Father said you would collect me.'

'No thank you. Not me. I'm a busy man.' Freeman turns to Ambition. 'Never just look at the negative, Ambition. Always consider the positive. Remember what I told you about learning how to propose?'

Ambition reluctantly puts the letter into his short's pocket.

'Tell her to give you a reply, okay?' Freeman picks up the handlebars of the wheelbarrow. 'Now, both of you jump into the ambulance and let's go and get the Sergeant before those bottle-store women wipe him clean of mother's pounds.'

Ambition and Ntando hop into the wheelbarrow, and Freeman pushes it up the road.

Chapter 30

Under the mango tree, Ngwenya has repaired his last shoe of the day, and he's preparing to go home. He fills two *shangani* bags with shoes, loads them on to his bicycle carrier and fastens the load down with a strip of rubber. He leaves the bicycle balanced against the tree and walks into the supermarket where he buys a bar of green soap and a loaf of bread – fortunately both are available.

He returns to the tree, where he finds that his load has fallen off the bicycle carrier. The rubber band has snapped. He replaces the load on the bicycle, and is just fastening it down again with a fresh strip of rubber when a wheelbarrow trundles to a stop beside him.

'*Baba!*'

'*Hawu baba.*' Freeman is still holding the wheelbarrow and the two boys look up, grinning merrily.

'Hello, boys. What are you doing here?' His mind is preoccupied with fastening his load. He has no more rubber strips, so this one has to hold.

'You're knocking off?'

'The sun has gone back to its mother, Freeman.'

Ambition and Ntando climb out of the wheelbarrow and stand staring at the figures dancing inside the bottle store.

'Have you seen my father anywhere around, Baba Ngwenya?'

Before the cobbler can reply, Nobuhle approaches them.

'My daughter-in-law,' Ngwenya greets Nobuhle.

Freeman glances quickly at Nobuhle, who's dressed in a tan blouse and khaki shorts. 'Hi,' he says, and looks vacantly over her head.

Nobuhle nods, her eyes also flitting from Freeman back to Ngwenya. 'Where's my husband?' she asks Ngwenya, smiling. The cobbler points at Ambition who's aping the movements of the dancers inside the bottle store with Ntando. 'See what they're doing,' he says, shaking his head, but smiling. 'Those two will grow up to be drunks, I tell you, my daughter-in-law.'

Nobuhle has a lean face with gentle lines and it creases into a mock frown. '*Haibo*, then how will he look after me?' She looks at Freeman. 'Your father is waiting for you outside your house. He told me that if I see you, I should tell you to bring the keys.'

'He's at home?' Freeman asks. 'We'd mounted a manhunt for him, me and my two soldiers. His people at work are looking for him.'

'He was here the whole day,' Ngwenya says. 'Then he went and came back again. He left just before you arrived. He was looking for his cell-phone. Maybe somebody stole it inside the bottle store. I saw Bra Ngeja was there at some point and we all know that one's story.'

'I have the phone.' Freeman takes it from his trouser pocket. 'My father was drunk. Ambition found him lying in a ditch and took the phone for safekeeping and then came to tell me. We brought this wheelbarrow to carry him home, but he wasn't in the ditch.'

'Don't talk like that about your father, my son,' Ngwenya says. 'In our culture we say an adult has eaten, *udlile*, but is not drunk.'

'But he's embarrassing us, Baba Ngwenya. And now he's wanted at work and how will he get there if he's eaten too much as you say?'

'Give him some strong black tea and he'll be all right,' Nobuhle says. 'You'd better hurry before he comes back to the bottle store and starts drinking again. Now I've got to go and find some sugar.' She turns and walks towards the supermarket. 'Coming with me?' she asks Ambition and Ntando.

'Come and make tea for him, Nobuhle,' Freeman calls out.

'He's your father, not mine.'

'But he's your father-in-law.'

Nobuhle turns and looks at Freeman with an expression that says 'Don't push this too far,' and she and the two boys disappear into the supermarket.

A smiling Ngwenya mounts his bicycle. 'Look after the boys,' he says to Freeman. 'It's getting late.' He cycles away.

Freeman sits on the wheelbarrow and lights up.

***

The supermarket shelves are almost bare and the shop feels empty as the trio walk up and down the aisles. 'What are you looking for,' Ambition

118

asks. He longs to be able to find whatever it is.

'Sugar,' says Nobuhle. 'I know they had a delivery of something this morning.'

Ambition stops in front of a bare shelf with a strip of paper sellotaped to the edge, which reads 'Sugar'. The price has been erased with a black felt pen. A male shop assistant with dreadlocked hair hovers in the aisle eyeing Nobuhle.

'When's the sugar coming?' Nobuhle asks.

'The day you learn to have a boyfriend in the supermarket,' the young man replies and snickers.

'Excuse me, what did you say?'

'You heard,' the young man replies. Nobuhle clicks her tongue at him in disgust, and he walks away whistling merrily as if nothing untoward has happened.

'Hope you didn't hear that.' Nobuhle says to her young companions. 'Some men have big holes in their heads.' She takes their hands and they walk to the till, where she buys two suckers.

'When will you be having sugar in the shop?' she asks the till operator.

'Nobody knows, and if we happen to get any, it'll be gone before you get to know about it.'

'Better learn not to use sugar, dear,' a woman behind Nobuhle says. 'My grandmother from the rural areas drinks her tea with salt. You must also try that.'

Nobuhle shrugs. 'And what will sugar cost when a sucker costs five thousand?'

Just as they are leaving, they are suddenly pushed aside by people running into the shop, their voices raised in panic.

'What is it?' Nobuhle's calls out. 'Ambition, stay here! Come back!'

But it's too late. A stone whizzes past Ambition's head and smashes into the sidewall of the entrance and shatters just as he steps out of the building.

Chapter 31

'I can't find Ambition,' MaNdlovu says to Ngwenya as he dismounts from his bicycle at the gate. 'I'm always telling him he must be home before it gets dark. And these days...' her voice trails away.

'Don't worry, he's with Freeman and Ntando at the shops. They should be here any time now.'

'Tshabalala has also been looking for Freeman. Right now he's sleeping on their doorstep.'

'Did he tell you he was looking for Freeman?' Ngwenya asks, pushing the bicycle around the house behind MaNdlovu. He remembers how Tshabalala had deliberately ignored him.

'I heard him asking Nobuhle at the gate.' MaNdlovu laughs softly. 'He was so drunk he could hardly stand upright.' She opens the back door while Ngwenya balances his bicycle against the wall by the door. Humming under his breath, he unties his two bags, carries them into the house and places them in a corner of the kitchen, which smells strongly of cabbage.

'You know I don't like cabbage,' Ngwenya says as he props his bicycle against the wall under their wedding photograph. 'Are the caterpillar worms finished?'

'You know the child doesn't like those worms. I can never seem to please you both.' MaNdlovu is carefully counting money out of an old stained bag. 'He ate very little in the afternoon, so I cooked the cabbage which I know he likes.'

'So tonight it's my turn to eat very little?' Ngwenya disappears behind the curtain into the bedroom. 'You'll spoil that child by making him so choosy about what he eats. When I was growing up, we had no choice about food; we ate anything our parents put before us.'

'That was then, and this is now. We can't have the child starve because we cook food that he doesn't like, but which his father does.'

'But still you spoil the children. What do they say, "Spare the rod and spoil the child"?'

'Well, you certainly don't spare the rod! Senzeni would be with us now if you hadn't beaten her, and beaten her without even asking for her side of the story! Do you call that justice? And do you think giving children the right food to eat is spoiling them?'

'*Hawu*, MaNdlovu, what's the matter with you today?'

His wife does not reply, but resumes counting her money. How can so many greasy notes add up to so little?

Ngwenya reappears, having changed into a pair of old jeans. Holding a towel and a piece of green soap, he pauses in the middle of the steamy room. 'Why didn't you buy more caterpillars if you knew they were finished?'

MaNdlovu points a finger at a metal dish by the wall that is full of *tshomoliya* . 'I didn't sell much today,' she says, her voice weary. 'You know there's now a communal garden and people are buying their vegetables from there because they're cheap. The little I sold will pay this month's subscription to the the burial society.' She points at one small pile of notes. 'And this is for the Christmas grocery subscription,' she says, pointing at the other.

'Sometimes I think we must do away with these subscriptions. We can live without them.'

'And if we leave the burial society and there's a death in the family, where are we going to get money to assist with the funeral? You know we've no savings at all.'

'Who says there's anybody who's going to die in the family?'

'Just look at what your daughter is doing now! I smell something frightening from that direction.'

'Do not say *your* daughter as if she is also not your daughter. And please let's leave that topic alone for now. I'm tired and I want to rest. Have you warmed my bathing water?'

'I'm still cooking, and this is a one-plate stove.'

'But what were you doing the whole day, MaNdlovu?'

'You're not the only one who works hard. If I'm not doing enough, why don't you take a second wife? There are plenty of women at the bottle store.'

'That's a good idea,' Ngwenya mutters, and goes out of the door.

***

Nobuhle grabs Ambition from among the melée of people on the pavement, with the intention of pulling him back into the safety of the supermarket, but then pauses. Two men are fighting in front of the building, surrounded by a cheering crowd.

Suddenly, one of the men breaks loose and picks up a stone. As he raises his arm an onlooker jumps on him, grabbing the stone and wrenching it away. They recognise Freeman, who yells, 'No!' as he pushes the two contestants apart. They are Mbambo, and the milkman, Peace, and it is Mbambo who had tried to throw the stone.

'Let them fight!' MaVundla calls from the door of the bottle store, raising her beer to her lips.

'No! Enough!' Freeman shouts again. He's a strong young man and he holds the two fighters apart. They're both breathing heavily, and it seems they are using the interlude to recover before attacking each other again.

At that moment, Peace steps sideways and kicks Mbambo in the chest. The cobbler falls backwards. The crowd roars. Mbambo leaps quickly to his feet, another stone in his hand and takes aim at the milkman, who ducks.

From the safety of the supermarket door, Nobuhle and her two charges watch as Peace dives toward Mbambo, and both men fall to the ground and roll. The crowd roars.

Now the milkman is on top of Mbambo, clobbering him on the head with his fist. 'Eyi! Eyi! Eyi!' shouts someone in the crowd. 'Finish him off, Peace!' MaVundla yells.

Then, to everyone's disappointment, two uniformed policemen arrive weilding truncheons. They each grab one of the two men and handcuff them.

'I gave him my child's school shoes to repair and he won't give them back!' the milkman shouts. 'He must've sold them. Do you know how much shoes cost? This guy's a thief!'

'He's lying, officer!' Mbambo retaliates, blood dripping from his mouth onto his shirt. 'He said something bad about the President and I told him I'd report him, so he started beating me up.'

The crowd gasps.

'That's a lie!' The milkman sounds shocked.

'It's a lie!' MaVundla intervenes. '3Pac's mad!'

'Who says it's a lie?' one of the policemen asks. No one answers.

MaVundla ducks back into the bottle store.

'Okay,' says the policeman. 'If it's a lie, let's go to the police station and you can explain yourself there. An insult to the President is an insult to us!' He turns to Mbambo, 'How can you, an old man, disgrace yourself by fighting?' He unlocks Mbambo's handcuffs and clips them onto his trouser belt. 'Go away and clean yourself up. We will deal with the bastard who's trying to undermine the authority of the President of our beloved country.'

'Will you need me to make a statement against him?' Nobuhle hears Mbambo ask.

'That will not be necessary,' the policeman replies. 'We have all the evidence we need.'

***

'Never go near people who are fighting. It's dangerous,' Nobuhle cautions Ambition and Ntando.

'3Pac was bleeding from the nose,' Ntando says excitedly. 'And he can't throw stones! Did you see that he missed somebody standing right in front of him? If it was a bird I'd have hit it with my catapult!'

'He's such a liar.' Nobuhle sounds angry. 'Now he's got the milkman into trouble.'

She turns to Ambition. 'I saw you the other day when the Green Bombers were chasing people down our line. You must promise me to run away when people are fighting.'

'One of them was Senzeni.'

'Would that have saved you from their stones?' Freeman asks as he comes up behind them, pushing the wheelbarrow.

'Mother wants her to come home,' Ambition says in a small voice. 'I wanted to tell her that.'

'This boy will grow up to be a real man,' Freeman says. 'He's so brave and he really cares about his sister.'

'Good for him.' Nobuhle looks sideways at Freeman, conscious that the young man had tried to stop the fight. 'But it's late now, so please take the kids back home. Ambition's mother must be looking for him, and your father is waiting for you, too.'

'Can I please buy you some chocolate first?'

'No thank you.'

'Oh, you're angry that Mbambo got that poor milkman into trouble

123

with the police? But that doesn't concern us.'

'Yes it does,' Nobuhle flashes back. 'What if it had been you?'

'If I tell you that the whole story starts with MaVundla would you believe me?'

'MaVundla?'

'Bottle store drama. I'll tell you one day.'

'No, tell me now.'

'Let's forget it, the story is not nice, especially towards women. ... Can't I buy you a Coca Cola, if you don't want chocolate? It's such a hot night.'

Nobuhle looks at Freeman for a moment without saying anything.

'Can I? Is that a "yes"?'

Ambition and Ntando stare at the young couple, sensing a tension they don't fully understand.

'No thank you,' Nobuhle replies. 'I prefer cold water, and there's plenty in the fridge at home.' She looks at the two young boys, 'Bye bye guys, you must go home now.'

Freeman stares at her as she walks away, a perplexed look on his face.

'Maybe she's already eaten,' Ntando offers consolation. 'Buy the Coke for us if she doesn't want it. Please, Freeman. Just one and we'll share it.'

'That's why you already have such a fat tummy, too many Cokes! What do you know about matters that concern adults?'

'You're not an adult Freeman. You're still a school boy!'

Freeman laughs. 'You're crazy Ntando. I'm a university man.'

At that moment, Ambition sees MaVundla coming out of the bottle store door looking very angry, and still with a bottle of beer. She walks over to Mbambo, who's gathering up his shoe repair equipment. Approaching from behind, MaVundla pours her bottle of beer over Mbambo's head. He turns to grab her, but MaVundla has already run away, and everyone on the pavement is laughing yet again.

Chapter 32

'MaVundla is a wild one,' Freeman says as they head for home, and bursts out laughing. 'She's the one who told me about the school shoes when I went to buy weed from her this morning.' He wipes tears from his eyes. 'She's my pal, and confides in me. Do you know what she did?'

Ambition is pushing the wheelbarrow as they turn into Sibambene Street. The tower lights are on, as it is after six and the sun has gone down.

'What did she say?' Ntando asks.

'She says that she took the shoes from Mbambo that morning when the Green Bombers were running wild. He owed her for something, and wouldn't pay. Afterwards she discovered that the shoes belonged to the milkman, who is also one of her customers. So she hatched the plan to make the two of them fight, because the milkman also owes her something! And bingo, she won today!' He laughs again.

The story is a bit too complicated for Ambition, but he doesn't query it. He remembered the altercation between Mbambo and MaVundla, but as for the rest... It has been a long day and he's tired.

Suddenly Freeman pauses. 'Say Ambi, did you give Nobuhle my letter?'

Ambition shakes his head. He'd forgotten the letter. It all seems such a long time ago.

'Don't worry. Just keep it for now. You can still do it later. Now it's my turn to push.'

***

Ngwenya sits on the sofa eating his supper while MaNdlovu sits on the bench eating hers. The sounds of the night intrude into the room: a car, a dog barking, a door banging closed.

'How was business today?' After their argument, MaNdlovu wants to break the silence.

Ngwenya does not reply immediately; then he says, 'If only Senzeni had been a proper child, in a few years time she would have completed her O-levels, and maybe gone on to do her As. After that, who knows, maybe college or university and she'd have found a good job.' He waves a tired hand around the room. 'Instead she's throwing stones at innocent people on behalf of a political party.'

'We also have Ambition, please don't forget,' MaNdlovu sighs. 'He will grow up to do everything we expected of his sister. And he's smart, always coming first in class.'

'It makes one wish we had given birth to him first. He could fulfil our dreams of having an educated person in the family to provide for us in old age when we're no longer able to look after ourselves.'

'I don't agree to that.' MaNdlovu answered firmly. 'It doesn't matter who was born first! We should have done more to see that Senzeni grew up as a more responsible person, even if she was not doing well in school. You should have tried to understand her instead of just beating her.'

Ngwenya sighs, not ready to rise to the provocation. 'Let me be honest with you, MaNdlovu. Do you think we will live to see Ambition succeed? I'm fifty-two now and you're what – forty-five – and Ambition has another eight, ten years left of school, assuming we live to pay for him.'

'My husband, you're tired, and you're sad. Senzeni has disappointed us, but only the Lord knows what will happen tomorrow. For now, let us just take good care of the boy and ourselves. The future will take care of itself.' She pauses, and then adds, 'And we must not give up on Senzeni, please.'

After supper, MaNdlovu collects the dishes and goes outside to wash them, leaving Ngwenya lying back on the sofa, his eyes half closed. A moment later he begins to snore. MaNdlvu returns with the clean dishes, casts a glance at her sleeping husband, and stacks the plates inside the cupboard. The clatter wakes up Ngwenya. He yawns and stretches.

'Did Tshabalala speak to you when you saw him at the gate?' he asks wearily.

'He only spoke to Nobuhle who was passing by.' MaNdlovu sits down again on the bench. 'You're worrying that he thinks we deliberately ignored him when we were going into the forest?'

'Yes.'

'But it couldn't be helped. We were on an important errand, and we were not supposed to speak to anyone.'

'But how could he know?' Ngwenya sighs again. 'And of all things, why did he choose exactly that moment to appear?'

'But even if he doesn't undersand why we didn't speak to him, we have no grudge against him. He will soon see that. If I see him in the morning, when he's sober, I'll greet him and he will understand.'

'He was at the bottle store the whole day yesterday and all today, and he didn't speak to me once, let alone nod his head in my direction. It was as if he was ignoring us as we ignored him.'

'There's also MaChivanda,' MaNdlovu adds. 'Remember she greeted us before we met Tshabalala, and we ignored her too?'

'I know. Have you seen her since yesterday?'

'I saw her in the street this afternoon, walking into the bush with a group of her church members, but I don't think she saw me.'

Ngwenya sits up, as he hears the sound of heavy footsteps walking around the house from the gate. MaNdlovu raises her eyebrows and he holds up his hand for her to be silent.

The footsteps stop at the back door, and they hear a heavy knock.

'Who is it?' Ngwenya calls.

'It's me, Baba!' Ambition calls, taking them by surprise, for both the footsteps and the knock had suggested a grown-up, not a child.

'Ambition, can you please stop playing games and come into the house at once!' MaNdlovu calls out. 'Can't you see what time it is now?'

The door opens, and much to their surprise, Tshabalala walks into the room in full riot uniform, carrying Ambition.

MaNdlovu gasps. 'What's the matter? Ambition, are you all right? Where have you been?'

'Good evening, good people,' Tshabalala greets them. His eyes are bloodshot under his helmet, and his face is tired, but he's smiling. 'I'm returning my hero.' He places Ambition on the floor.

'Your hero?' Ngwenya replies, looking confused. MaNdlovu puts a hand on her son's shoulder.

'I drank too much this morning and passed out in a ditch,' Tshabalala says with a laugh, and a whiff of stale alcohol fills the room. 'And now Freeman tells me that Ambition found me, took my cellphone for safekeeping, and then walked home to tell Freeman where I was. Just imagine that.'

'Well done, my boy!' Ngwenya smiles with pleasure.

'The cellphone could have been stolen, so I don't know how I can thank this good child.'

'Please take a seat Baba Tshabalala,' MaNdlovu says. 'Can I make you a cup of tea?'

'No thank you, I'm not staying long.'

'Ambition is your child as well, Tshabalala.' Ngwenya says proudly.

'Quite right,' Tshabalala agrees. 'But I've just been called back to work, although it's supposed to be my night off and I could do with a good sleep.'

'Is there any problem?' Ngwenya asks cautiously. Any hint of political trouble in the township is always a source of tension and anxiety for Ngwenya and MaNdlovu, knowing that it must involve the Green Bombers, and therefore Senzeni.

Tshabalala frowns. 'These stupid elections are causing unnecesary suffering – and for what? Can somebody please tell me?' He shakes his head despairingly. 'Good night, good people. I'll see you tomorrow. Please stay strong.' Ngwenya shakes his hand and closes the back door behind him. Like Tshabalala, he feels that nothing good can come of these elections.

'Is this a time to be out in the streets, Ambition? You did well, but how many times have I told you to be home before dark!'

'Don't scold the child,' says Ngwenya. 'He did well. We were only talking about Tshabalala before he came.'

'I was with Freeman.' Ambition takes his mother's hand; he can sense the anxiety in the room, which has displaced the earlier moment of warmth and comfort. 'We were looking for his father. Father saw us at the shops, didn't you, Baba?'

'Since when have you started looking for lost people?' MaNdlovu asks, before Ngwenya can reply. She's frowning, but there is a smile in her eyes. 'What if you get lost yourself? Who is going to look for you? Now go and wash your hands at the tap and come and have your supper before I throw it out to Ginger,'

'Well!' Ngwenya lets out a deep breath. 'At least one problem's been solved.

'I told you Tshabalala is a good man, even if he does work for the police.'

1978

Chapter 33

The war still raged around the countryside, and some farms near Wildberg Ranch had been attacked and their main houses destroyed. Strangely for anyone who was not in the know, the guerrillas always skirted Wildberg Ranch. And it had been during the rainy season in November of that year that Mrs Phillips had given Thenjiwe a two-week vacation, saying she wanted her to be around over the Christmas period, as she was expecting visitors from South Africa.

So, she had been gladly making her way home after an absence of seven months when Samson had suddenly materialised in front of her.

'What are you doing appearing suddenly like a wild animal?' she had scolded him. 'Do you want to give me a heart attack?'

It had been a beautiful day, the morning sky was clear and the ground damp and rich-smelling after the previous night's rainstorm.

'I'm going to Jiba too.'

'You're lost then,' Thenjiwe had told him, smiling. 'Your home is in Tsholotsho, in that direction.' She pointed northwards.

'Who said that I was going home? I am hoping to accompany you to yours!'

'Samson, if you've nothing better to do, please get out of my way, I've a long distance to walk before nightfall.'

'But I'm coming with you, Thenjiwe, and if you don't want me to walk with you, then I shall simply follow behind.'

She suddenly realised that this was not the Samson with whom she was used to cracking jokes on the ranch house veranda, and she felt her breath catch in her throat, as if she'd been startled by something.

'Okay, let's go then,' she said steadily, though her heart was pounding. 'A man should walk ahead, so that if wild animals come upon us, they eat him first! Remember, there are wild buffalo around here.'

She had meant it as a joke, but Samson had not laughed. He had just looked at her, and picked up her suitcase.

They'd walked for almost an hour without having any real conversation – she didn't remember saying anything to him, or him saying anything to her. Then he'd stopped under a *mopane* tree, placed her suitcase on the ground, taken a handkerchief from his pocket, and stepped closer to her. Without asking for permission, he'd gently wiped the sweat from her face. She'd made a half-hearted gesture to ward off his hand, but she knew what he was doing, like a man who has planned something for a long time.

'There's drinking water in the suitcase,' she told him, 'you can rinse the handkerchief and wipe your face too.'

She remembered that they had sat resting under that *mopane* tree for a while, both drowsy from the heat and fatigue. And then Samson had begun to speak: 'Ever since that night we hid together in the gulley,' he whispered, 'and I slept with you in my arms, I fell in love with you. For months I have dreamed of you becoming my wife.' He took her hand in his, and his palm was rough, that of a man who works hard. She knew that as his fingers massaged her palm, he also felt the strength of her hands. They were capable of holding together a household. 'I love you, daughter of Ndlovu,' he told her.

She remembered that she had been moved, and touched, but also confused, and so she'd said, 'But I regard you as a brother, Samson!' which was, she knew, both true and untrue.

'That's good,' he'd replied. 'Because it shows you trust me as you would trust one of your own blood, but I can never be your brother, only the father of your children.'

'We must hurry,' she said, 'or we'll get caught in the rain.'

He'd picked up her suitcase and they'd continued on their journey.

They'd walked for several hours more, just keeping ahead of the steadily darkening clouds. When her home was in sight, he'd stopped and placed her suitcase at his feet.

'I was joking about coming with you to your home,' he told her. 'But only for today, because if I enter now, I will do so as a brother or a friend; and, as I told you, I want to be more than that.' She'd not replied, but stood in front of him staring at her feet.

'I shall wait for you to return to the ranch, and then we'll start planning how I can present myself to your parents. Goodbye.' He turned to go, and she knew that he had hours to walk back to the ranch, and no doubt through the pouring rain.

MaNdlovu remembered her sense of rapture. Was it just that she was wanted, or the sense of a new future, or that she felt more herself for being loved and respected? She would become Samson's wife.

2004

Chapter 34

He was walking into the school toilet. The walls and the air are as grey as a faded picture. His footsteps have a muffled echo; his ears feel as if they are blocked with water. He's scared of the toilet, its mysterious rows of tiny cubicles, its emptiness, the chemical stench of dip, but his bladder is near to bursting. He reaches the urinal – and jerks awake. Slowly, he feels the blanket beneath him. It's dry. His bladder is burning.

He gets out of bed, gropes his way along the wall and switches on the light. He looks beside the sofa, but he's forgotten to place the plastic container he uses as a pot there. Still not quite awake, he switches off the light.

He turns the lock carefully, making sure it does not make any noise, so as not to alert any goblins outside. He pokes his head out into the night. The darkness is softly lit from the tower lights, and a few stars wink at him, as if sharing some mischief. Nothing seems to be waiting to gobble him up in the yard.

He stands on the doorstep, contemplating relieving himself right there, but he knows that a damp patch on the ground will alert his mother when she sweeps the yard in the morning.

Fearfully, he steps away from the doorstep, leaving the door open, and walks across the yard to the *delele* hedge on Ntando's side of the yard, and pees, listening to his water pattering against the leaves. Although it was hot inside the house, the night is cool and a slight wind rustles through the air.

Turning, he jumps in fright as an animal appears through the hole in the hedge. It's Ginger, and he's carrying something furry in his mouth. He runs past Ambition, who follows, curious to see what the dog is carrying. Goblins are now the furthest thing from his mind.

He walks to the front of the house, but Ginger is nowhere in sight. He walks to the gate, and sees the dog disappearing into the hedge of a house across the street. He looks down the street, just as a group of people emerge from the shadows at the end of it. Under the tower lights, he sees them running hard towards him.. As Ambition watches, the leader stops and points a finger at a house, and the group all throw stones at the windows.

There is the sound of shattering glass, then they run towards Ambition, and the leader points at another house, stones are hurled again, glass shatters and the group runs on past Ambition's home and then stops and looks back. Ambition swallows hard. He has ducked behind the hedge, but can they see him? The group mill around behind their leader.

'This one also?' The speaker slowly lifts his right hand and points towards Ambition's home. Terrified, Ambition hardly knows what he is doing as he rises naked from behind the hedge and steps into full view.

'*Ntikolotshi!*' a voice yells, and the group bolt away in dissaray. Ambition is shivering, partly with fear, partly because he suddenly feels very cold, very exposed. There's someone standing alone in the street.

'Ambition!' he hears the whispered shout, 'What are you doing outside the house after midnight?' It's Senzeni.

Heaving a sigh of relief, he calls, 'I'm watching you.'

'Stark naked?'

'Yes'

'You really are a strange kid. My friends now think you're a goblin. Did mother see you leave the house?'

'No.'

'Then go back inside quickly. Things are bad tonight.'

'Let's go in together.'

'You go!'

'I don't want to. You found me outside.'

Senzeni steps nearer and lays a hand on her brother's bare shoulder. 'I miss you,' she says in a low voice.

'We also miss you,' Ambition replies. His sister's hand is warm on his skin.

Senzeni steps back. 'You miss me?' There is disbelief in her voice.

'Yes, we miss you. Please come back home, father and mother have forgiven you.'

Senzeni snorts. 'It's too late. I've been promoted and I'm going away to work in the rural areas until the elections are over. We're going to win the elections and when I come back, I will be having a good job and I am going to find a place of my own to stay where nobody is going to give me any rules. How can my own parents say I don't have a mind just because I was getting bad marks at school? They don't know anything!'

'Don't go, Senzeni,' Ambition says softly. 'You have a mind and we all love you at home.'

There's a moment of silence.

'I don't believe you. Has Freeman been making you smoke weed?'

'I'm serious, Senzeni. You have to come back home. This is where you belong.'

Senzeni looks over Ambition's shoulder as a light comes on in their house.

'I'm going,' she whispers. She sounds as if she is about to cry. 'They don't love me! Father doesn't love me. Look how he used to beat me!'

'They love you, Senzeni!'

'And do you know why I stole mother's underwear that day?' Senzeni is speaking very fast, but still in a whisper. 'I took it because I wanted to sell it and raise money for you to go to that Matopo Hills school trip that mother had said she couldn't afford.'

'You shouldn't have done that, Senzeni.'

'You're so *stupid*! Couldn't you see I was doing it for you? Mother bought that underwear from MaVundla on the very day she refused to give you the money for the school trip. I thought that was unfair...' her voice breaks again.

'Ambition!' MaNdlovu calls. Senzeni pats Ambitions's shoulder, turns around and runs into the night.

MaNdlovu emerges wrapped in a blanket. Ngwenya follows behind in a pair of cut-off jeans.

'What are you doing outside the house at this hour, Ambition?' Ngwenya sounds both angry and shocked.

'Nothing.' Ambition shivers.

Just then, Bra Ngeja appears, walking fast, with a plasma TV firmly balanced on his shoulder. He walks past their gate without looking and disappears in the direction of his house.

'Where are your clothes?' MaNdlovu asks.

'In the house. ... I just came out to pee Mama, I was pressed.'

'Why pee at the gate, so far away from the house, and at this hour?'

'And who were you talking to?' Ngwenya asks, still sounding angry. 'I clearly heard two voices, but you're alone.'

'It was Senzeni. She was with the Green Bombers who were throwing stones at the houses across the road. Tomorrow you will see that the windows are smashed.'

'Oh dear Lord Father.' MaNdlovu's voice is despairing.

Up and down the street, lights are switched on and people in various states of semi-dress are streaming out of their gates.

'Take the child back into the house, quickly!' Ngwenya commands his wife, but before she can move, they hear a piercing scream.

'That's Mrs Nkani,' Ambition says in a small voice.

'I don't like this,' Ngwenya shakes his head. 'MaNdlovu, please take the child into the house. I'll go and see what's happening.'

A stricken look fills MaNdlovu's face. 'Don't go, Ambition's father. Please come back into the house with us.'

'I have to find out what's happening. And besides, people will ask questions if they see us out here and we don't go to help.'

'But you heard Ambition saying that Senzeni and the Green Bombers are somewhere nearby.'

'Yes! And that's why I need to find out what's going on.'

The sound of angry, anxious voices floats towards them. A child begins to cry.

'Please go into the house with the child, MaNdlovu. Now!'

'Okay, if that's what you want, but how will we know if anything happens to you? I don't want to spend the whole night worrying. I've done that before, remember!'

'Nothing's going to happen to me, I'm near my home and there are many people around.'

Reluctantly, MaNdlovu takes Ambition's hand and they walk towards the house.

Ngwenya walks towards the first group of people standing outside a house with shattered windows and glass all over the yard. When he reaches them, they fall silent, and stare at him accusingly.

'What's happened?' Ngwenya asks, though he knows full well.

No one replies.

The silence is suddenly broken by MaVundla, who shouts, 'Police!' No one needs to be told what to do – everyone disappears into their own homes. Ngwenya also turns back towards his gate, feeling the dark cluster of the police foot patrol behind him, and the continuous sound of the woman who is wailing.

Once inside the house, he closes the door, turns the key, and releases a deep breath.

MaNdlovu is standing beside Ambition, who is already tucked up in his bedding. Ngwenya turns off the kitchen light.

'What is it?'

'Shhh!' Ngwenya's voice hisses in the darkness. 'The police!'

Ngwenya parts a corner of the curtain and peeps outside. He can see the patrol approaching, and he can feel MaNdlovu's anxiety. There's the hiss of a police radio, the police pause, he thinks he can hear muttering, and then they turn and walk away.

'Are they gone?' MaNdlovu whispers.

'It seems so.'

Ngwenya takes another quick look outside.

'Why was that woman wailing?'

'I don't know. I didn't hear. No one would speak to me.'

Chapter 35

In the morning, Sibambene Street is strewn with leaflets, which only add to the sense of confusion and disarray. 'What do they say?' Ntando asks Ambition as they jog along the street. They've been sent by Freeman to buy a packet of cigarettes and he's told them to hurry.

'It's difficult English.' Ambition tries to read a leaflet as they run. 'We'll ask Freeman when we get back.'

'Ah, shame,' Ntando says, pointing to a house across the street with smashed windows. A woman, the one who recently moved into their line, is fastening a piece of cardboard over one of the broken panes with sellotape, while her son stands by. On this side of the street, they walk past Mbambo's house, and it's untouched.

'Look,' Ntando points again, '3Pac's windows aren't broken.'

'Maybe he was playing Tupac's *Thug Life* when the other windows were being broken.'

'And why don't the thieves break the doorlocks instead of the windows?'

'Go and ask Bra Ngeja,' Ambition replies. 'The windows of his house aren't broken either, but maybe you'll find cuts on his arms. I saw him carrying a TV down the street last night. He must've stolen it.'

'And why were you outside in the middle of the night?'

'I don't eat chicken heads like you, *mfana*! If I did I'd also sleep early.'

'But, I still don't understand...'

'Ah... let's stop talking about it now. I'm tired from running.'

He doesn't know how to answer Ntando's questions. He knows, everyone knows, that the windows were broken by Green Bombers, but a kind of loyalty to Senzeni keeps him silent. He just doesn't feel he can answer all the questions that would follow if he told Ntando, though he can't understand why he doesn't know already, his father being a police-man, and his brother being a man with his ear to the ground.

'Mama sent us a new DVD player and some DVDs from the UK,' Ntan-do says, happy to change the subject. 'Baba says if Bra Ngeja comes and steals it, he'll beat him up with his truncheon ... like this!' The small boy whips the air with a fist.

'Good for you.' Ambition puts his hand on Ntando's shoulder to slow him down. 'Maybe Never-Say-Never will copy new dance moves from the movies – that style of dancing with a bottle on his head is old now. Tell me, how did a grown-up learn to do that? Even I can't do it.'

'Maybe you can't dance because your father can't dance. Baba says it's because he's poor.'

'He said what? That's an insult!'

Realising he's upset his friend, Ntando backtracks, 'Well, he said it last night when he came back from work, but he also said that your father is a good man, a good cobbler, and he likes him.'

'And your father is also a good man ... although he's a ZANU-PF po-liceman.'

'But he's never brought a gun home, and I want to hold a gun to see what it's like.'

'Don't be stupid, you know a gun can explode and kill you.'

'Don't worry, Ambi. You're my friend, and if my father brings one home I'll call you to come and touch it too.'

The two boys walk past Lotshe Street, and turn into Zobohla, when they see Nobuhle walking their way.

'Where are you two off to so early?' Nobuhle looks tired, as if she's al-ready walked a long way.

'Where did you get that sugar from?' Ntando asks.

'Black market! But only after walking around the whole township.'

'What's a black market, my Dictionary?' Ntando looks at Ambition.

'A place that's not a white market!' Ambition doesn't have a clue, but he thinks this answer makes sense.

Nobuhle smiles. 'Silly you! Is that what they teach you in your class? And what position did you come out in class last term?'

'He was number one!' Ntando interjects before Ambition can reply, his eyes twinkling.

'Really? Well done.' Nobuhle smiles, 'And last year in Grade Four you also came first, didn't you?'

Ambition, embarrassed, is drawing circles on the ground with his toe. 'But he can't read these papers!' Ntando hold up a leaflet.

'I can!' Ambition says hotly. 'But I don't know the meaning of all the words. They're difficult.'

'Too right,' Nobuhle says comfortingly. 'You shouldn't be surprised. They're meant for grown-ups. But please throw them away – if the Green Bombers catch you with them, you'll get into big trouble.'

'But what do they say, Nobuhle? Are they using bad language like on Freeman's DVDs?'

'No, no, it's not bad language,' Nobuhle explains. 'The leaflets are written by the MDC, and they say people should vote for their MDC leader. Just throw them away.'

Ambition's eyes follow the flight of the leaflets, which sail through the air, and waft to the ground, adding to the litter already decorating the streets. He can hear his mother telling him to *always* use the litter bin, and feels a bit ashamed, though now it is too late to pick them all up. They'd done what Nobuhle told them to do.

It's then that Ambition remembers Freeman's letter, and he takes it out of his pocket.

'What's this, Ambi?' Nobuhle looks at the letter being proferred. 'You've written me a letter, my husband?'

'It's from Freeman.'

'What does he want that he can't come and tell me?' She takes the letter and begins to slit the envelope, hears a noise and looks up.

Down the street come two policemen, accompanied by MaChivanda in her usual church robes and Bra Ngeja, who's carrying a TV set. A group of boys follow behind, booing. Suddenly MaVundla appears from behind MaChivanda and lunges at Bra Ngeja, hitting him hard on the side of his face; MaChivanda quickly follows her example and gives Bra Ngeja a good hard kick on his bottom. The children scream with excitement as one of the policemen tries to push the two women away.

MaChivanda shouts heatedly, 'He's a thief and he must be beaten!'

'No, Mama, the law does not allow people to beat other people,' a policeman says. 'Just leave this matter to us, we know how to deal with it.'

'What's the matter, MaChivanda?' Nobuhle asks as the group passes them, though the matter is as clear as daylight.

'I've just caught him red-handed.' MaChivanda is very angry. 'He broke into my house last night and stole my TV from the sitting room.'

'*Yebo?*'

'Luckily, Ambition's mother saw him carrying the TV. She guessed it was mine, because of its size, and alerted me this morning when I told her that someone had broken into my house. I called the police and we caught him sitting watching *my* TV in *his* house – imagine stealing from a neighbour!' Nobuhle shakes her head.

'Today his *muti* ran out. The police will take care of him!' MaChivanda picks up the skirts of her robe and runs after the policemen and Bra Ngeja.

'It's unfair.'

'What's unfair, Ambition?' Nobuhle asks.

'When the Green Bombers beat people up, the police don't do anything; when they break people's windows, they don't do anything either, but now they arrest a thief. What's important, the lives of people or TVs?'

'It's a good question, Ambi, but thieves must be caught as well. Keep your ideas to yourself for now, though. You never know who is listening. You're a clever boy, and we don't want you beaten up.'

Ntando taps his foot impatiently. 'We have to go now. Freeman said we must hurry'

'Please wait a minute more, ' Nobuhle asks. 'Let me read the letter first.'

She takes the letter out of the envelope and begins reading it. Ambition watches MaChivanda, who has rejoined the police group and can't help trying to kick Bra Ngeja, though the police keep trying to stop her.

Ntando is watching Nobuble closely. 'What does he say?'

'Mind your own business!'

When Nobuhle's finished the letter, her face is expressionless. She looks at Ambition. 'Tell Freeman I'll visit him this afternoon when his father's gone to work.' She looks pointedly at Ntando. 'But tell him that we'll meet under the peach tree outside the house. Okay, *mfana*? Now I have to go.'

'Let's hurry,' Ntando says to Ambition, 'or Freeman will be mad, even if we have a message from Nobuhle.'

'You really wanted her to meet your brother inside the house, didn't you?' Ambition says. Ntando starts giggling, but before he can reply they see Ambition's father turn into the street in front of them. He's walking very fast.

'Where are you going to?' he asks as soon as he sees them, as if expecting bad news.

'Freeman sent us to the shops for cigarettes.'

'Has your mother left to sell her vegetables yet?'

'I left her cleaning the house.'

'We must all go home now.'

'What about Freeman's cigarettes?'

'He'll have to go to the shops himself,' Ngwenya says wearily.

Chapter 36

When they arrive, MaNdlovu is sweeping the kitchen. Seeing her husband and the two boys close on his heels, she looks worried. Ngwenya brushes past her without speaking, throws himself on the sofa, and sits staring at the ceiling. Ambition and Ntando sit down side by side on the bench.

'Your silence scares me.' MaNdlovu feels a knot of panic in her stomach. Something's happened.

Ngwenya sighs. MaNdlovu says gently, 'Ntando, will you please go home now?'.

The little boy's face falls, and he puts his head on Ambition's shoulder.

'I'm not chasing you away, Ntando. I'll call you back soon, okay?'

'Take Freeman's money back to him, Ntando,' Ngwenya adds. 'Tell him I'm sorry Ambition can't go to the shops right now. We'll call you later to play with Ambition, okay?'

MaNdlovu closes the door behind Ntando and sits down.

'*Uhambe njani?*' MaNdlovu asks quietly.

Ngwenya raises his head, and takes a deep breath. 'Mr Nkani is dead,' he says flatly.

'Oh no!' MaNdlovu gasps.

'It's said he was beaten up last night by the Green Bombers when he tried to stop them stoning his house.'

'No! Please God, no!'

'A report about the murder was made at the police station last night by Mrs Nkani, and she told the police who the culprits were.'

'Have they been arrested?' MaNdlovu feels a mounting sense of dread.

Ngwenya shakes his head. 'The police told them that it was not the Green Bombers who killed him, but thieves who were trying to rob his house.'

'And Senzeni?'

'I've been to the Ilanga Youth Centre to look for her. There's no one there. They've all left. It's as if nobody has ever lived there.'

'Last night she told me she'd been promoted and was going to work in the rural areas,' Ambition says in a small voice.

Ngwenya stares stonily at his son, though he is looking somewhere beyond him. 'What do the Green Bombers mean by "work"?'.

MaNdlovu is weeping. She feels her heart will break.

Ambition looks at his father, tears are streaming down his face too.

Something breaks inside Ambition. He cannot bear to see his parents crying. Their pain engulfs him, and he buries his head in his mother's lap.

'I am here,' a small voice says from the bedroom doorway.

***

Ambition had no words to describe the feeling that swept over him when he heard that voice. It was like an electric charge; he shuddered and looked up.

His mother's hands tighten around him. Tears are running down her face but she's stopped weeping.

Senzeni is standing at the bedroom doorway, holding the curtain aside. She's wearing her cream T-shirt and the matching skirt. Ambition's eyes move between his father and his sister. Ngwenya is looking at Senzeni too, frowning as if he cannot believe it is her. The room is filled with silence. His mother looks both disbelieving and fearful.

'Have you come back, Senzeni?' Ambition breaks the silence.

Senzeni looks up. Her cheeks are rivers of tears. Suddenly, she starts moaning, a sound that comes from somewhere deep inside her, and throws herself at her mother, who reaches out to catch her. Senzeni is crying helplessly.

'I have come back home,' she sobs. 'Please can I stay?'

'This is your home,' MaNdlovu croons. 'Hush my child. You are home now.'

'They killed Mr Nkani,' Senzeni says, her chest heaving. 'They hit him with stones while I was talking to Ambition at our gate. They killed him, Mama. So I came back here in the morning. I came through the back while you were sweeping at the front, and I have been lying under the bed.'

'Stop crying, Senzeni,' Ngwenya's voice is firm. 'You've done the right thing and no one is going to punish you for it.'

MaNdlovu puts one arm round Senzeni's shoulder and the other around her son. She cannot quite believe that the nightmare is over. It has happened too quickly. But with her son and daughter beside her, she feels very comforted.

Ambition suddenly jumps up. He needs action to relieve all the tension.

He quickly slips through the hole in the hedge. There's no one in Ntando's backyard. He runs across it and slips through a hole into MaVundla's yard. MaVundla is standing at her back door with Power and giving him a pair of black school shoes.

'Go to that milkman's house and throw these shoes into his yard,' she tells him. She spots Ambition. 'Ambi,' she calls, 'where are you going in such a hurry?'

Ambition pretends not to hear, and slips through the fence into Mbambo's yard. It's still quite early; usually at this time of day Mbambo's radio will be pumping out music, but his house is cloaked in silence.

There's a window beside the back door, and Ambition presses his face to the glass. The room is empty. Shoes are scattered all over the floor, among them a black balaclava, crumpled like a deflated football.

'What *are* you doing, Ambition?'

His father, mother, Senzeni and MaVundla are all standing behind him 'I just wanted to see if Mbambo is still here.'

'Why would you want to do that?' His mother's brow is furrowed with concern.

'He was the one who was making the Green Bombers do what they did,' Ambition says simply.

Everyone stares at him. MaVundla speaks first.

'I think Ambition could be right. I saw that moron loading his things into a police van when I was coming from the bar, and off he went. I don't think he's going to be coming back very soon.' She pauses. 'I'd had a few drinks so I didn't think too much about it at the time.'

'Mbambo has gone with the militia,' Senzeni tells them quietly. 'Let's go back home and I'll explain everything.'

***

Ambition and Ntando are lying on their stomachs peeping through the hole in the hedge. On the other side, Freeman and Nobuhle are sitting in the shade of the peach tree chatting quietly. Suddenly, Freeman leans over towards Nobuhle and kisses her. Ntando giggles, and a voice behind them asks what they're doing.

It's Senzeni, in a pretty yellow dress, with her hair freshly plaited. Ambition and Ntando leap to their feet, laughing, and make a run for the corner of the house.

Senzeni watches them, smiling.